NEAR STRANGERS

WINNER OF
THE 2023
AUTUMN HOUSE
FICTION PRIZE

NEAR STRANGERS

stories

MARIAN CROTTY

AUTUMN
HOUSE PRESS

Pittsburgh, PA

Near Strangers
Copyright © 2024 by Marian Crotty
ISBN: 978-1-637681-00-8
Published by Autumn House Press
All Rights Reserved

Cover and book design: Joel W. Coggins
Cover photo: Darren Sacks / Stills.com

Library of Congress Cataloging-in-Publication Data

Names: Crotty, Marian, 1980- author.
Title: Near strangers : stories / Marian Crotty.
Other titles: Near strangers (Compilation)
Description: Pittsburgh, PA : Autumn House Press, 2024.
Identifiers: LCCN 2024020430 | ISBN 9781637681008 (paperback ; acid-free
  paper) | ISBN 9781637681015 (epub)
Subjects: BISAC: FICTION / Short Stories (single author) | FICTION /
  Family Life / General | LCGFT: Queer fiction. | Short stories.
Classification: LCC PS3603.R6797 N43 2024 | DDC 813/.6--dc23/eng/
  20240513
LC record available at https://lccn.loc.gov/2024020430

This book was printed in the United States on acid-free paper that meets the
international standards of permanent books intended for purchase by libraries.

Autumn House Press is a nonprofit corporation whose mission is the publication
and promotion of poetry and other fine literature. The press gratefully acknowledges
support from individual donors, public and private foundations, and government
agencies. This book was supported, in part, by the Greater Pittsburgh Arts Council
and the Pennsylvania Council on the Arts, a state agency funded by the Common-
wealth of Pennsylvania.

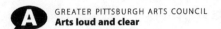

GREATER PITTSBURGH ARTS COUNCIL
Arts loud and clear

pennsylvania
COUNCIL ON THE ARTS

TO MELISSA
AND EVERETT

CONTENTS

NEAR STRANGERS

HALLOWEEN

My grandmother Jan had fucked-up ideas about love. This was something anyone who had spent about five minutes with her understood. She had been married three times—once to my grandfather and twice to a guy named David who I remember as a quiet gray-bearded man with a motorcycle, who had also broken into her duplex and set fire to the wicker patio furniture that she'd always kept in her sunroom. When I asked if she'd been afraid of him, she shrugged. "Sure. Sometimes." In her mind, love was an undertaking that required constant vigilance and bravery, and when she spoke about her relationships, I often thought of a woman I had seen on YouTube trying to explain why she had been raising the tiger cub that eventually mauled her. "We loved each other," the woman said. "I don't expect anyone to understand."

But when it came to Erika, the girl who had recently broken my heart, after what was admittedly just one relatively chaste summer together, Jan was my ideal audience: sympathetic, almost always available, and the only person in my life who thought that getting back together with Erika was both advisable and likely to happen.

"You're beautiful," she would say as if this settled the matter. "Look at you! This girl is obviously having cold feet. Maybe she's just not ready to be gay."

The logical part of my brain thought the more likely explanation was that Erika had only gotten together with me in the first place out of boredom and convenience. We had spent the summer working together at a frozen yogurt shop called Yotopia! and now that FSU was back for the fall semester, it embarrassed her to be with a high school student. Sometimes, though, in the midst of one of Jan's musings, I could almost convince myself that there had been a misunderstanding and that if I could just show Erika I was a mature and attractive person, she would, if not see that she had made a mistake, at least consider making out with me in secret.

"When it comes to love," Jan said, "you shouldn't have regrets. I have regrets, and I can tell you it sucks. I never should have divorced your grandfather."

It was a Saturday afternoon and we were walking along a paved path through a leafy park on the east side of town. During the week, it was mostly used by dog walkers and runners, but now the playgrounds were crowded with little kids, and under one of the covered pavilions a family of loud, happy people was having a birthday cookout for someone named Bianca. Jan walked very fast and we were both a little out of breath. She had told me this story many times. My grandfather was a decent and hardworking man who, after years of Jan threatening divorce every time he drank too much or came home late from work, had finally called her bluff. As a result, her life had been lonely and difficult for the past forty years.

"If you have a chance to set things right," she said solemnly. "The least you can do is try."

/ / / / / / /

Jan was my dad's mom, but he, along with his two older sisters, had a strained relationship with her. Partially because of the yelling and chaos from their childhoods and partially because of what they called her "attention-seeking tendencies"—buying Cuisinart mixers and flat-screen televisions for people she barely knew, walking out of my cousin Trent's high school graduation party because she felt ignored by his friends, requesting an apology from my aunt Kelly for not having been invited to visit her newborn twins in the NICU. In large groups, especially, Jan often made provocative statements inspired by daytime television and the youthful coworkers she knew from the various crappy retail jobs she held. "Maybe I'll go and get my stomach frozen like I heard on Dr. Oz," or, "Now, what do you think it would be like to be married to Kanye West?"

My mom, though, who had only officially been Jan's daughter-in-law for about a year after I was born, invited her over to our house any time there was a special occasion or holiday: Christmas, Thanksgiving, Easter, birthdays. Jan had babysat when I was little and my mom had no money for daycare, and so, as far as she was concerned, Jan was family. When my mom's mother complained that she would like just one "family-only holiday," my mom would smile sweetly and tell her she was welcome to visit another time. It was only after it was just the two of us that my mom would let herself flop on the couch with a glass of wine and shake her head about a cayenne lemon water diet Jan was trying for unspecified reasons or a horror costume involving a fake dead baby that she'd worn to a children's Halloween party. "My God," she would say. "What do you think goes on in her head to make her act that way?"

\ \ \ \ \ \ \

That fall, my grandmother was living in a new and supposedly high-end apartment complex that came with a gym, a garage parking space, a gated entry that required a code after 9:00 p.m., and a twenty-five-yard outdoor swimming pool that was heated in the winter and where we spent at least two evenings a week together. I was avoiding my mom's boyfriend; Jan was trying to distract herself from the job she'd recently lost at Nordstrom and her fear that in her seventies she was too old to get hired anywhere else. The other residents were almost all college students and young professionals with seemingly endless amounts of time to splash around at the pool half naked, drinking beer out of thermoses and playing rowdy games of volleyball, but that didn't stop Jan from doing her water exercises, which involved wearing a wide weighted belt she'd bought off QVC and moving through the water in a way that looked kind of like moonwalking and kind of like a person feeling around in the dark for a lost object. I didn't have an exercise belt and so would borrow one of the apartment complex kickboards and glide along beside her while she gave me advice about Erika and listened to me complain about my mother's boyfriend, who, all of a sudden, after about two years dating my mom, seemed to be around constantly. His name was Pete, and he was a social worker at the hospital where she worked. He was a thin, very pale man with wispy yellowish hair and wire-framed glasses that were always flecked with grime. He was in his early fifties, about a decade older than she was, and divorced with two kids in college. He was relentlessly polite to me and kind to my mother. I hated him.

"He's too skinny," I would say. "And have you heard the way he coughs? In another ten years, she's going to be taking care of him."

I also didn't like the way he ate—too quickly and with appreciative, almost sexual sounds, how he was always fiddling with his beard, how every single one of his hobbies—nature walks, invasive plant removal, pickleball, historical biographies—seemed like contests at withstanding boredom. Jan didn't seem to have any issues with Pete, though I thought she usually gave men too much credit, including my father who had followed a woman to Charlotte when I was two and had been absent for most of my childhood. But she let me complain and would admit, at least, that his clothes were terrible. Clunky orthotics worn with tall white athletic socks, multiple colors of pleated chinos in the same unflattering style.

"That's fixable, though," Jan would say. "If your mom wants to put in the work. Men are just like that. They always need a lot of help."

My mother, along with her sister, her friends, Jan, and basically every other woman we knew who was over thirty-five, seemed to think that she was lucky to find Pete—a single, employed guy who thanked her for all of the nice things she did for him and who didn't mind that she had just turned forty and had a kid. The fact that I was the only one who seemed to notice that she was about a thousand times better looking than him or that she was always the one cooking dinner filled me with a sense of righteous indignation, though, on some level I knew that no matter who she dated, I would see him as a trespasser.

As for Erika, Jan's main advice was to wear revealing outfits and to behave as if my life without her was surprising and wonderful. I should be friendly in an easy, casual way that showed I didn't need her, and I certainly shouldn't ask her to go out with me again.

"Of course not," I said, though in fact, I had called and texted Erika so many times in the past two weeks begging her to reconsider that she had blocked me on social media and was now switching shifts at Yotopia! to avoid me. I understood exactly how pathetic this made me look since it was approximately the same way that my ex-boyfriend Nick had reacted when I'd finally broken up with him in July after I'd already been messing around with Erika for two months. But I was having trouble controlling myself. Being around Erika electrified my skin, my body, the air in the room. Didn't this mean *something*?

"When do you work together again?" Jan said, squinting up at me while she bobbed along the deep end. "Find out and look good that day."

"Okay."

"And remember. Easy breezy. Lemon squeezy."

"What?"

"You don't know that one? Customer service 101. If you feel yourself getting moody or sentimental, you just chant that in your head, and it'll get you back on track."

/ / / / / / /

The next time I was supposed to work with Erika, she got her shift covered, but I saw her again the following Friday night. She worked the back cash register by the drive-through and I worked up front with the face-to-face customers. Because of the three-for-one Decadent Shakes promotion, which I was pretty sure the owner, Gina, was losing money on, we were slammed—families with kids, college students, a Little League baseball team along with about a dozen of their parents and coaches. There wasn't much I could do to look nicer; we all had to wear latex gloves, khaki aprons, and teal polo shirts with the company logo on the pocket—Yotopia! and a swirl of pink yogurt that looked like smoke rising out of a chunk of kiwi—but I decided to take Jan's advice and tried to seem happy and outgoing.

Wooing the customers wasn't too complicated—you just smiled at their kids and offered them free samples—but being within a few feet of Erika made me queasy and stupid. There was her dark hair tucked behind her ears, her pink, slightly puffy lips, the tiny circle tattooed on the inside of her wrist. While I made Decadent Shakes and parfaits and refilled the yogurt machine, my head swam with all of the possible things I could say to her but then whenever there was a brief lag between customers, I wasted it. Finally, around eight thirty, things slowed down and we both found ourselves up front, sneaking crushed-up candy bars from the topping bins with tasting spoons and doing just enough side work to look busy. I was sweeping; she was wiping down tables. I knew that if I didn't say something soon, I'd miss my chance.

"Hey, can I ask you something?" I said finally.

She looked up at me from the plastic shield over the display freezer that she was wiping down with Windex.

"Okay."

I could tell she thought I was going to ask why she didn't love me or why, given our obvious chemistry, she hadn't actually slept with me, but the truth was I hadn't yet decided what I was going to say. I thought about apologizing for harassing her or suggesting friendship. I wanted to work St. George Island into the conversation, so she'd remember the afternoon we'd spent there with our coworkers, the two of us lying side by side on a beach blanket, nearly touching. Making each other crazy until we'd snuck away to a changing room in the women's bathroom, wet sand everywhere, shivering out of bikini tops. But then I thought of Jan chanting *Easy Breezy Lemon Squeezy* and took a different tack.

"Why do you think there were five cherry-flavored Skittles in the urinal?"

Erika squinted at me a little, but her face softened, and I could see that she was going to play along. "How do you know they were cherry-flavored?"

"Aren't the red ones always cherry?"

"Yeah," she said. "Maybe." And then a few minutes later, she nodded at the tip jar out front, which we would split at the end of the night, and told me I was on a roll.

"Nice work, Jules," she said. "The people love you."

I shrugged. "Decadent Shake special."

Pretty soon after that, we hit another rush, and it stayed too busy to say much else to each other, but something had shifted between us. The ice had broken and though things weren't exactly normal again, Erika no longer seemed like she wanted to avoid me. When I reported back to Jan later that week, she said, "Of course it worked. Why wouldn't it have worked?"

\ \ \ \ \ \ \

After that Friday night, Erika stopped giving away so many of her shifts, and for the next month or so, I got to see her two, sometimes three, times a week. It was my senior year and I was busy with the AP math and science classes that I'd taken in hopes of getting a scholarship to one of the liberal arts schools in cold, unfortunate cities like Grinnell, Iowa, or Richmond, Indiana, where my guidance counselor thought other students might not want to go. Working, especially when Erika was there, began to feel like a break from worrying about the future. Where would I go to college? How would I pay for it? What would my life be like if—*when?*—I went away to school and my mom and Pete moved in together? His house was nicer than ours—a creaky two-bedroom, buried under a thicket of live oaks and pollen that always smelled damp. He lived on the very edge of Betton Hills, which was the fanciest neighborhood in Tallahassee, in a small bright ranch house with new counters and appliances, a slate roof, and pink azaleas out front, but even though I knew it was babyish to feel this way, the thought of moving out of the house I'd grown up in made me want to cry.

At work, all of this disappeared behind the swell of pop music and the rush of customers. When Erika was there, I tried to demonstrate how likable I could be: chatting and flirting with customers, smiling so hard my face hurt. At school I barely spoke to anyone but my friend Paloma and never managed to talk in class without my entire chest and face going hot and red, but at Yotopia!, no one seemed to guess that this friendly, confident person was a lie. That you could just decide to be a different person, that you didn't have to actually change to convince people, felt like a revelation.

In the lulls between customers, Erika told me about how her parents were pressuring her to major in marketing instead of studio art or to, at the very least, pursue an internship they'd found at an insurance company through one of their South Florida accountant friends. She thought this was selling out, but she was worried about being broke. Usually, I didn't add much about my life because it was boring and because I didn't want to say anything that would remind her that I was in high school, but I did sometimes talk about Nick who was eager for me to admit I was bisexual.

"I think he thinks me being gay makes him a virgin or something," I said one day. "He's seriously freaking out about it."

I tried to make it seem like my relationship with him hadn't mattered, but I knew this wasn't true. There had been three years of inside jokes, flash drives of indie music slipped into each other's book bags. He had told me that he'd peed his bed until he was seven, that his father had made him quit soccer because he was slower than the other kids, too embarrassing to watch; I told him that I collected photos from social media of my dad who, according to his wife's page, *was* a good father to his new family in North Carolina but just not to me. Nick and I had made out and given each other orgasms and lain naked in his bedroom many times before the spring of our junior year when we'd finally had sex, and all of this, too, had seemed like easy, uncomplicated happiness. Now, though, in comparison to Erika, nothing with Nick felt real.

"Well, it's probably hard for him," she said. "But that doesn't mean you have to be the one to listen."

\ \ \ \ \ \ \

By October, the awkwardness between us had all but gone away, but it was also making me crazy to be around her. Paloma thought I should quit my job and concentrate on getting into a good liberal arts school, which would undoubtedly be filled with lesbians who were even hotter and cooler than Erika; Jan said I should make up another girl who had a crush on me and look for reasons to casually touch Erika.

"Does that actually work?"

"Oh yes," she said. "At least on men. Remember Gabriel?"

"No."

"Yes, you do. He looked like a chubby George Clooney. Dark hair and a beard. We almost got married."

I didn't remember him but nodded.

"I fixed his tie on a Tuesday and by Saturday I had a date."

I wasn't fully convinced about this plan, but I also knew that Froyo season was coming to a close and that Gina would probably stop scheduling two people on weekdays.

The next time I saw Erika, I started a group chat with three of my classmates about chemistry homework and grinned stupidly at my phone every time it lit up with a reply. Finally, after about two hours, she asked what was happening.

"Nothing," I said. "Probably nothing. I met someone at Lake Ella and now she's texting me."

Erika smiled in a way that seemed a little forced.

"She wants to teach me how to skateboard."

"Are you going to go?"

"Maybe."

"Is she cute?"

My face burned. I wasn't used to making things up, and it felt dangerous and unsavory. It was hard to believe the lie wasn't obvious. I looked down at the tile floor between us, sticky with dried pools of frozen yogurt and covered with napkins and little bits of candy, nuts, and fruit smashed into the grout.

"Good for you, Julie," she said. "Text her back."

"Maybe," I said. "I don't know if I feel like it."

Two hours later, when the store closed, I found Erika in the supply closet, lined with tall wire shelves where we stocked the dry goods and paper products, reaching for a box of latex gloves. When I slid behind her, I put my hand on her back and asked her to throw down a box of paper towels. Except for a dull amber light bulb, the closet was dark.

"I already changed those," she said. "Both bathrooms and the kitchen."

"Okay, thanks," I said, but I didn't move my hand.

"Also, you shouldn't touch me like that."

I stepped back and she turned to face me. There wasn't much space in the supply closet and we were maybe a foot apart. She had taken off her polo shirt and was now wearing an FSU T-shirt cut up into a tank top that showed the sides of a black sports bra.

"I'm sorry—" I said, but then she turned toward me and brushed my hair away from my face with both hands and then we were kissing. Fast and hard, more breathless than it had been before. I slid my hands under her shirt and against her back; she pulled me against her and grabbed my butt. I thought, *If she tries to take off my clothes, right here, I will let her,* but then we heard Gina arrive to count the money and lock up, and Erika stepped back. I thought she was going to tell me she regretted it, that she'd made a mistake, but instead she squeezed my hand. "Let's clean up and get out of here, okay?"

The next half hour of side work was a slow, delicious ache. Erika looking over at me, blood thrumming in my ears. It was happening finally—the two of us—though I wasn't exactly sure what *it* was. All summer she'd treated me more gently and carefully than I'd wanted. We'd make out, roll around half naked, but if I reached for her pants, she'd stop me. Tonight, though, things felt different. Was it possible that Jan knew how to make someone fall for you?

After work, I followed her outside to the parking lot of the strip mall, walked in step with her without talking. The door to the laundromat two doors down was open, and the smell of bleach wafted out onto the sidewalk. The Indian food market had closed for the night but still the neon flamingo in the window advertising Florida lottery tickets blinked. At the corner by a defunct car wash, cars slowed for a stoplight. When we got to my sun-bleached Corolla, I said, "Are you going to take me somewhere?"

"Is that what you want?"

"Yes."

She looked at me for what felt like a long time.

"Okay," she said, finally, "I'm texting you the address."

She'd left the sublease where she'd spent the summer and was now living in a gray shotgun house on the other side of town with little potted plants everywhere and a brown leather furniture set that I'd never seen before. The kitchen and living room were dark, but I could hear music behind a closed door in the other bedroom. Erika told me to wait in the living room while she changed her sheets, and I texted my mom that I was hanging out with a friend and would be home late. It wasn't even a lie exactly, but my mom didn't like Erika, and I felt bad for not telling her the whole truth.

A few minutes later, Erika appeared in the archway between the living room and the hallway, and I followed her back to her room, which was painted electric blue and covered in small framed art prints. I took off my shirt first and kissed her, and then we were tangled on her bedspread in our underwear under her slowly rotating ceiling fan.

She kissed me and ran her hands along my body. "You're shivering," she said. "Are you cold?"

"No." I felt impatient and dizzy. She had leaned away from me and was propped up on an elbow.

"We don't have to do anything else," she said. "You know that right?"

I pulled her on top of me, slid off my underwear. "Come on," I said. "Stop talking."

The rest was a blur of nerves and adrenaline until we were done, and I was lying in the crook of her arm, the length of her body against mine. Time slowed down, and I felt as if I were floating. If nothing else happened between us, I knew that this moment was enough.

/ / / / / / /

That Monday afternoon, she texted to say that she'd gotten the marketing internship. She was quitting Yotopia! and didn't want me to hear about it from someone else. Also, she'd had a good time with me on Friday but didn't think we should do it again. Hopefully I understood.

Not really, I wrote back.

Are you mad? she texted.

No.

Do you regret it?

No. Do you?

The gray text bubbles of ellipses appeared and disappeared.

Then she texted back, *No.*

Although I wanted more than anything to guilt her into seeing me again, I knew that I'd only gotten to have sex with her in the first place by playing it cool. *I'll see you around, I guess* I wrote back. *Maybe we can be friends.*

To this Erika responded almost immediately that she was sorry but, no, she couldn't be my friend, although she wished me well.

Stupidly, I felt fine, maybe even good. I had found someone perfect, and she had slept with me. The fact that she had done so against her better judgment just proved that she was attracted to me in the same combustible way I felt for her, and attraction like that seemed rare and true, a tugging magnet that couldn't easily be ignored. Eventually, maybe in a year, maybe in several years, it seemed possible we'd find our way back to each other.

\ \ \ \ \ \ \

Less than a week later, I was at Yotopia! when Erika stopped by to drop off her polo shirts and aprons. She was wearing tight jeans and a flannel shirt rolled up at the sleeves, showing off a thick-banded watch she always wore. Just the way she walked made my stomach swish. It was midday on a Monday, but school was closed for parent-teacher conferences, and I could see that she was startled to see me. She waved and then walked over to Gina who was doing paperwork at one of the tables out front. I could make out the gist of their conversation—good luck at the internship, come back if you ever need a job. Erika had worked there for two years, and Gina seemed genuinely sad to see her go. Then she peered out the window at Erika's car, where a pretty girl in mirrored sunglasses leaned against the bumper. "Is that Kat?"

Erika nodded. I couldn't hear what she was saying, but my heart was pounding. Kat was Erika's ex-girlfriend, her first true love. Were they back together? Gina knocked on the window. Kat waved. Gina motioned for her to come in, and she put her phone in her back pocket and walked toward us. She was wearing very short jean shorts with the pockets hanging out under the fringe, cowboy boots. She was thin but curvy with long shiny brown hair, big boobs, and smooth muscular legs.

I took a drive-through order and when I came back to get the frozen yogurt, Gina was behind the counter, making two chocolate-vanilla swirl cones. Kat was sitting across from Erika, legs stretched out under Erika's chair, and Erika was talking to her, but also looking up at me, watching me in a deliberate way that was supposed to communicate something—that she was sorry, that she hadn't meant for me to see her with Kat? I wasn't sure, but it was a guilty, pitying look, and I pretended not to notice. Gina handed them the cones and then the three of them chatted for another ten minutes before Kat and Erika stood up with their half-finished cones and left. They were walking across the parking lot, side by side, close but not touching, laughing about something, and all of a sudden, I understood. Kat might have spent the summer elsewhere, but there had been no breakup—all spring, all summer, while I had been falling in love with Erika, they had been together.

"That front door's covered in dog drool," Gina said. "It needs to get wiped down."

/ / / / / /

Paloma said that Erika was an asshole who deserved no more of my time or attention and that if I couldn't stop myself from thinking about her, I should make a list of her flaws. This was what she'd done with her ex-boyfriend Christian, and now she barely thought about him at all.

"I can't think of anything," I said. "Everything supposedly bad about her I like."

"She lied to you. She's twenty and into a seventeen-year-old. She has a girlfriend and a dumb haircut. She's not that good at art—"

"Okay," I said. "Please stop."

We were at school, sitting on a brick wall outside the cafeteria, eating lunch. The lingering heat and humidity were finally giving way to cooler fall days. Across the lawn, a plastic bag sailed in the breeze.

Paloma took a bite of her sandwich and then lifted her sunglasses and squinted at me.

"Do you feel sick? Like physically?"

I nodded. All week it had felt like how I imagined a drug withdrawal might feel—nausea, weakness, a lack of will to do anything but sit very still and cry.

"It gets better, I promise," she said. "You just can't let yourself contact her again or the wound doesn't heal, okay?"

\ \ \ \ \ \ \

Jan had gotten a job at a pop-up Halloween costume store in the lesser, and mostly defunct, Tallahassee Mall, so I was spending more time at home. Because of this and because Paloma was sick of hearing about Erika, I told my mom about Erika and Kat one morning while the two of us were folding laundry. I left out the part about us hooking up as well as my Jan-inspired campaign to win her back.

"I know you didn't like her," I said. "So now I guess you'll say I told you so."

"Oh, come on, Jules," she said gently and put her hand on my knee. "You know I don't think that. Is this why you've been sad?"

I nodded.

"I'm sorry, honey," she said. "I hate that this happened."

To her credit, she didn't say anything else. She just hugged me and let me talk. That night we got candy at Publix, ordered pizza, and stayed up late like when it was just us, making fun of Lifetime movies until we couldn't keep our eyes open.

A couple of days after that, though, Pete was over for dinner and said, out of nowhere, that breakups were hard, that even when he spoke to veterans and refugees and people who'd suffered great trauma, the issues they invariably came back to were about love.

"As humans we're wired that way," he said. "Don't let anyone tell you a breakup's not a big deal."

If he hadn't looked so pleased with himself, I might have let it go.

"I guess we don't have secrets anymore," I said to my mom.

She looked like I had punched her, which I suppose was what I had intended, though on some other level, I was just naming the truth. Pete was now her confidant, and as much as she deserved to have him, I had once been her entire family and all she ever seemed to need.

/ / / / / / /

On Halloween I was with Jan, watching television and waiting for trick-or-treaters who probably were not going to come, when I got a text from another Yotopia! employee inviting me to a Halloween party at Erika's house. I knew that I wasn't *actually* invited, but I was still considering going. "I shouldn't, right? Probably that would be a horrible idea . . ."

"Yes," Jan said. "But I understand why you would want to go."

"But I shouldn't, right?" I repeated.

She reached for a mini Snickers and then smiled at me the way teachers did when they refused to give you the answer. "You're practically an adult, Jules," she said. "If you want to go, I'm not going to stop you."

When I told her about Kat, she'd said that she'd never cheated but had been the other woman a few times and that she'd let things happen with David that should not have happened. That she was a person who understood how, in the name of love, you could do things that seemed foolish. David had been very jealous, had followed her around, gone through her purse. She'd been a cocktail waitress at the time and he'd been convinced that she was flirting with other guys. I thought, but didn't say, that this sounded sad, that she'd been in her sixties at the time and should have known better.

Now, she said, "You know about the furniture, right? About David trying to burn down my house and kill me?"

I nodded, though I'd never heard it put that way.

"Nobody knows this and don't tell your mother," she said, "but I was with him after that for almost a year."

I sat very still and tried to look normal. On the television, a commercial for auto insurance gave way to a cartoon cat dancing in a tray of kitty litter.

"I don't regret it either," Jan said. "To be with the person you want is heaven. It doesn't have to be the right circumstances to feel good."

This was the opposite of what sounded true, the opposite of why my mom had told me she was with Pete. She loved him, yes, but the more important thing was that he was devoted and dependable, that he didn't jerk her around. I knew that Jan sounded crazy and that it made no sense for me to crash a party where a girl who had not only mistreated me, but also made it very clear she didn't want to see me anymore would be hanging out with her girlfriend, but I also knew that I was going to go. I wanted to be in this same room with her, and I wanted this helpless feeling to go away. To imagine a lifetime of this feeling made me dizzy.

"I just want to be around her, I guess," I said. "That's all."

Jan handed me a box of Halloween costumes she'd gotten on discount this fall.

"Go for an hour," she said. "Wear a mask and don't say anything. I'll drive."

NEAR STRANGERS

Betsy had a feeling she'd get a call tonight, but it's still disorienting when it happens. Four in the morning, pitch-black. She had a glass of chardonnay last night, too, which has left her foggy-headed. You aren't supposed to drink when you're on call, but she had her neighborhood anti-racism meeting on Zoom and needed wine to tolerate Jill, the high-strung, condescending woman who leads the group. Plus, she's seventy-three years old. If she wants a glass of wine, she's not going to ask permission.

"There's a SAFE call," the voice on the line says. "Can you take it?"

SAFE stands for something—she can't remember what exactly—but it means someone's been raped, and she will go to the hospital to give them clean underwear and run interference with the police.

"Okay, yes," she says. "I'm on my way."

On her first few calls, she would rush out the door, but now she knows better. She takes a moment to brush her teeth, make coffee and a sandwich, find an extra sweater.

Outside, the air has the slight chill of early fall, and the neighborhood is nearly silent but bright. Long shafts of silvery light sweep down from the streetlights and clouds of artificial white light hang over each stoop, one after another on every row house. Lighting up your whole yard while you sleep was an actual suggestion printed in the neighborhood newsletter to prevent crime, which, as far as she can tell, is pretty much nonexistent. The neighborhood is solidly middle-class these days, filled with anxious strivers—all of these professors and lawyers crowded into their redbrick row houses for the local elementary school, then outfitting their 1,200 square feet with open-concept kitchens and finished basements, big decks and flower beds of tiny manicured rose bushes. "A culture of fear and surveillance" is what someone in the anti-racism group said in the Zoom meeting a few weeks ago about the so-called Citizens on Patrol, but when she said this applied to the local obsession with floodlights, Jill acted like she was senile. "The lights are to see at night, Betsy," she said. "I think that's pretty standard."

The drive to the hospital is just over a mile and through residential streets so quiet she can drive as cautiously as she likes. She passes a soccer field, a bus stop, a giant industrial cube of a building that belongs to the university. She likes spying on the world this way, having a reason to be awake at these odd hours, the sense that she's doing something both secret and important.

Zaid has not asked her to quit volunteering, but he worries about her being out alone at night and in a hospital in the midst of a pandemic, so she's considering it. She is under no illusions that she is irreplaceable or even particularly good at this work. Other than being reliable, her strengths are just that she is willing to talk back to the police, and, because she was once a language arts teacher, she is good at the paperwork. She helps the women put their stories in order, gets them to include the details that will mean something to a prosecutor. *He restrained me* will become *He held down my arms and left a bruise on both wrists. He threatened me* will become *He said he'd punch me in* my *"fucking ugly face."* Both at the hospital and at the courthouse, where she helps with the paperwork for protective orders, the women fixate on the wrong details—the personal betrayal instead of the crime. *He gave away our microwave just to piss me off* a woman once told her at the courthouse but nearly forgot to mention the time this boyfriend had tried to drown her in a bathtub. If she quits, she'll miss it, but she would gladly give up a lot of things for Zaid.

Zaid is her son Andrew's ex-husband, an engineer who lives in Raleigh with his new husband and their children, who keeps in touch with Betsy even though her own son doesn't speak to her. They separated eight years ago, around the time Andrew stopped coming home for Christmas but a couple years before he cut her out of his life completely. Then, a few years ago, she had an abnormal mammogram and, in a moment of loneliness and terror, wrote a vague Facebook post asking for prayers, and Zaid called to wish her well.

"I wasn't sure if it was okay to call you," he said on her voicemail. "But, you're family. I think about you a lot, in fact, and I hope you've been okay."

She had been so shocked by his message—frankly, she was surprised he was still her Facebook friend—that it had taken her nearly a month to call him back, but then they'd talked for over an hour. He told her about his new job procuring chemicals for a steel company in Raleigh, the two brothers he and his new husband adopted from foster care. He didn't say, though she suspects it's true, that this version of his life is the real one, that all of those years with Andrew were simply a tense and unpleasant false start.

These days, he calls her regularly and hosts her in Raleigh over the holidays and kids' summer vacations, where she is always surprised by his cluttered house of LEGO sets and IKEA units, how different it is from the stylish high-rise condo of amoeba-shaped coffee tables and Italian sectionals that he shared with Andrew. He's different, too, sillier and more openly affectionate. A man who makes Mickey Mouse pancakes, chases the kids with Nerf guns, reaches for his husband's hand at the dinner table. But around him, she is cautious; she doesn't understand his generosity, it's hard to trust it.

At first, she suspected he'd reached out to her to punish Andrew, but when she asked what he thought of the two of them staying in touch, he seemed embarrassed. "I don't talk to Andrew," he said gently. "I wouldn't know how to reach him if I tried." She now thinks his kindness has something to do with his culture's respect for old people—he was born in Pakistan and moved to the States in middle school—and with his parents, who have maintained a relationship with him by pretending he is not gay. Or possibly, like her, he is just lonely.

The one tricky part of the drive is right before the hospital when the road widens and curves at the same time and suddenly becomes six lanes instead of four. Past the curve, there's a stoplight and then a median that appears out of nowhere, and it's nearly impossible in the dark to stay in the correct lane. She slows down for the turn, and then there's a car behind her, beeping for a long angry time.

"All right, Dale Earnhardt!" she says out loud. "*What* is your problem?"

The car, an older white Honda Accord, swerves around her and takes a left into the main entrance of the hospital, stops at the ticket counter, and then speeds off. She imagines a medical emergency or that the driver might be a sleep-deprived nurse, so tries to "send them goodwill" as the Pilates woman at the YMCA used to say, but the flare of anger stays in her chest. "You're not wrong to feel those things," her therapist had once told her, "it's the size and duration of your reactions that we need to work on." But how to make that pulse of rage go away? How to hear an insult without adding it to the collection of small hurts you'll carry around forever?

She parks in the big parking deck with everybody else—no discount just for being a volunteer—and she goes through the automatic doors to the front desk, where a slight Black woman in pink scrubs and a burgundy wig checks her ID and pushes a button to make heavy metal doors swing open. At the nurse's station, nestled at the end of a fluorescent bleach-soaked hallway, a beefy redheaded man has a corded phone to his ear and manila folder open on the desk in front of him. When she identifies herself, he points to a plastic chair in the hallway.

"She's getting her exam?"

He shakes his head without making eye contact. "Not here yet."

He means the SAFE nurse who is trained to collect evidence without retraumatizing anyone.

"It shouldn't be long," he says and points again to the chair.

She expects him to say more, but he goes back to his paperwork, and she thinks, as she often does, how much people reveal about themselves when they talk to old people. Anti-racist Jill, for instance, interrupts her in a high-pitched irritated voice at every Zoom meeting, but then there is that attractive young couple in the group, Maddie and Austin, who will stop a vote to ask what she and the other old lady think. "I'd like to hear from some of the longer-term residents," Austin will say. "Betsy, Catherine, can you speak to the history on this issue?" Often, she doesn't have much to add, but just hearing his young, earnest voice acknowledge them in that way shoots a surge of joy through her whole body.

She moves the plastic chair away from a heating vent and sits down across from the closed door with its plastic flag flipped forward to indicate it's in use. The exam rooms are always the same—thirteen and sixteen, two private rooms with bathrooms used only for these cases and tucked away from the rest of the patients—so that survivors, this is what they are told to call them, can't be harassed by their assailants.

"That happens?" she asked in the training. She imagined a rapist running through the hallways, ripping open exam curtains, and it felt like the plot of a bad movie.

The leader of the training shrugged. "A lot of bad things happen. In this line of work, there aren't a lot of surprises."

The training had been eight hours a day for five days, led by a series of overworked social workers at the women's shelter in a small conference room where a picture hung of a former resident who'd been shot in the head by her ex-husband, handwritten tributes from the other residents scrawled on the matting under the frame. That week has stayed sharp in her mind the way everything from that spring does. Andrew had just cut off contact completely, and although it wasn't a total surprise, she had found herself so stunned and grief-stricken, she'd wound up in therapy. *How did it come to this?* She'd cry in the woman's office, going over the same events and conversations, trying to make them add up to a life without her son. How could it be that the little boy who had followed her around their house "helping" her dust and mop and bake banana bread, who'd woken her up each morning by putting his nose against her nose, had grown up into a man who hated her?

"You're so stubborn," he'd told her once, back when his anger had seemed temporary. "It's like you're incapable of ever admitting you were wrong."

He'd never forgiven her for cheating on his decent if self-involved father, but his biggest grudge involved a Johns Hopkins student named Sean Bursten who he'd been sleeping with when he was sixteen. As soon as she'd found out about Sean, she'd located his parents in the phone book and asked for their help ending the relationship. This, according to Andrew, had set in motion a series of tragic events that began with the parents' refusal to continue paying for college and ended with the boy's suicide a year later.

"You outed him to his homophobic parents," Andrew had accused years after the fact. "He's basically dead because of you." He had just finished his first semester at Duke and come home for Christmas, filled with a righteous anger that he'd never expressed before.

"You were sixteen and he was twenty."

He stared at her blankly.

"But are you *sorry*? Do you regret what you did?"

She hesitated. She had felt so blindsided by the whole situation that she hadn't been thinking clearly. There had been the age difference, the secret meetings, and yes, the fact that Andrew was gay, which at the time had felt like proof that he was a stranger to her. And yet, she had also genuinely been worried for his safety, and what was it exactly, that she should have done?

"I regret what happened, obviously—"

Then he was walking away from her, slamming each door he passed on his way to his bedroom, and that was the last time they'd spoken about Sean.

The therapist was the one who suggested she volunteer and when she'd shown up to that first training, she'd been resistant. She was not a do-gooder kind of person, and she didn't see how pretending to be would help. There had been about a half dozen participants, including an EMT from western Maryland who'd said her coworker had joked that if you went to a training at a women's shelter, the other participants would all be lesbians.

"My son is gay," Betsy said automatically and then seeing the woman's face immediately regretted it. She hadn't meant to scold anyone; she'd just wanted an excuse to talk about Andrew, which made him feel close to her even though he wasn't.

"My partner is an idiot," the EMT said. "*That* was the only point I was trying to make."

When the door to room thirteen opens, she's expecting a medical staff person to emerge, but it's two police officers—a no-nonsense woman in her thirties with an auburn bob who Betsy has worked with before, fine, if humorless, and a short athletic blond guy who looks like he's about twelve. Usually they get here after Betsy, and if not, they are supposed to wait for her unless the survivor tells them not to.

"Excuse me, I'm the advocate," she says and stands up. "Did somebody tell her she can have an advocate before you asked her questions?"

She says this nicely, but the male cop flushes. In addition to their uniforms, they are wearing masks and plastic eye coverings that look like snorkeling goggles, and his has left red indentations across his face and forehead.

"She knows," the female cop says. "She didn't have much to say to us anyway."

"Okay."

"She had them call it in," the male cop says, "but now she doesn't want to cooperate."

He says this without any apparent anger, but Betsy bristles. Why should this woman have any obligation to him at all?

"This was a bad one," the female cop says, voice low, a look on her face of a person who's been told to show compassion. "Unknown assailant, lots of violence. It would be good if she can help us catch him."

Helping the police is not Betsy's role here, and frankly, not a major goal in her life generally, but if you don't help them, they make things worse for everyone. In the situations in which a woman has chosen not to report, it has more often than not been a reaction to their insensitivity. "They act like *I'm* the criminal," one woman had told her and then she'd left before she had an exam.

"I hear you," Betsy tells the police officers. "I'll do what I can to help."

In the training materials, they were told that violence can happen to anyone, anywhere, but the truth is there are patterns. Almost all of the survivors are women, usually under forty; the assailants are typically men these women know. Contrary to what Betsy had suspected, the women are not usually college students but tend, in fact, to be from worlds she never thought too much about. They live in cars or homeless shelters or apartments shared with many other immigrants or in a house that belongs to a family member and is filled with multiple generations. They wash dishes, cook in cafeterias, clean airplanes in the middle of the night. They've been raped in drug houses, their own bedrooms, an ex-boyfriend's couch, a patch of littered grass behind a Safeway. Hearing their stories fills Betsy with a sense of astonishment that this is what the world is like, that these women have survived it. She is relieved when someone arrives from a life in which this horrible thing seems to be an anomaly.

The woman in the exam room has limp bleached hair that's grown dark at the roots, a delicate gold necklace around her neck, a cupid's arrow tattoo on her wrist. She's wearing a faded blue and white hospital gown and has bruises blooming on her face and neck and collarbone, a gash on her face that's being held together with tape. She looks like someone who's barely survived a major car accident.

"I'm Betsy," she says. "The advocate from the women's shelter."

She adjusts a blue surgical mask that likely covers more damage. "I think the police are pissed at me."

"Don't worry about that," she says. "Now what's your name?"

"Lenna. Lenora, but everyone calls me Lenna."

With the exception of her quick-moving brown eyes, she seems exceptionally calm.

"Okay Lenna. First question, do you *want* the police to be here?"

"I don't know."

"That's okay. Take your time."

Betsy takes out two Ziploc bags—one that contains soap and other personal care products to be used after the exam and another filled with snacks. The idea is not just to provide what is needed but to give a person who has been violated the chance to choose for herself. M&Ms or crackers? Gatorade or water?

"I'm not hungry, but I'd take some deodorant," she says. "I smell like shit."

She gives a half smile and then frowns. "Sorry."

"You can say *shit*," Betsy says and hands her a squat travel-size stick of Secret. "Say whatever you like."

She tells Lenna that the nurse will arrive soon to give her Plan B and other prophylactics, and if she wants, will do an exam to collect evidence and document injuries. She has a year to report and can have the evidence collected anonymously if she hasn't decided what she wants to do.

"Can't I stay anonymous and have the police still go look for the guy?"

Betsy hesitates. Theoretically, this would be possible, but she's never seen it happen. A lot of times even when the women *do* report, the cases get dropped.

"Unlikely."

"I don't even live here really," Lenna says. "I can't see myself coming back for a trial."

"A lot of cases don't go to trial," Betsy says. "But I understand. Whatever you decide is okay."

Betsy has about five pages of paperwork to complete for the women's shelter, which will be used to compile data and to follow up with Lenna. She skips the questions about the assault and asks for the demographic information. The list of questions reveals that she is twenty-three and has been living in her parents' house in Lutherville, a middle-class suburb of strip malls and subdivisions on the other side of the highway, where she argues with her parents about politics and applies for jobs she doesn't particularly want. In her life before the pandemic, she was a waitress and dancer in New York.

"I was in a few musicals," she says. "Things had actually been going pretty good."

Betsy recalculates this girl's look not as white working-class but as twenty-something artist. She had thought, because this had been the case with another woman, that dancer had been a euphemism for stripper.

"You must be good."

She shrugs and then seems to reconsider. "Yeah, I guess so."

She's willing to share a cell phone number but not an address since she's not planning to tell her parents.

Betsy hesitates. "That's fine," she says, though she's not sure Lenna has thought this through. If she goes home with a face like that, she'll have to have a story.

"They're not scared of the virus. They don't trust the news," Lenna says. "I told them I was going to the movies with friends tonight, and they thought that was fine."

Betsy nods. "My neighbor had a birthday party for herself, and I watched about two dozen people go into that house without masks. It's terrifying."

"They're crazy," Lenna says. "They never used to be like that."

Betsy feels herself wanting to follow this tangent, but the nurse will be here any minute, and she needs to keep them on track.

"So, you weren't at the movies?"

Lenna shakes her head. She seems to want to continue but doesn't, so they sit in the artificial light in silence. Outside the door, she hears the muted sounds of voices and carts being wheeled by.

"Whatever you were doing, it wasn't your fault, you know. I don't care if you were walking around naked."

She has said these sentences so many times they have become a cliché, but the women often need to hear it. Even in a completely random attack, they blame themselves, which she suspects is a way for them to find a reason for why it all happened. If they know what they did wrong, they can make sure not to do it again.

"Worse," Lenna says. "What I was doing was worse."

Betsy stays quiet and does her best to radiate kindness, and eventually, seeing that Betsy is not going to fill the silence, Lenna starts talking.

"I have sex with this guy from Tinder."

Betsy nods in what she hopes is a friendly way. "Okay."

"Do you know about Tinder?"

She has to smile at this. "Yes."

"Okay, so we have sex at night in a car or sometimes a park. You know, for airflow or whatever because of the virus. We've been meeting up since this summer, but I don't even know him. We don't, you know, talk."

She seems embarrassed to say all of this, but Betsy doesn't think it is so embarrassing. She has her own stories of car sex with Buddy Phillips, the sweaty graying married civics teacher she was drawn to simply because he stared at her breasts in faculty meetings. The affair itself was short-lived but clarifying—the last bit of proof she'd needed to know that her marriage was over. Since the divorce, she's had her share of boyfriends and casual sex, a couple of one-night stands as recent as a decade ago that she knows would shock her friend Helen. To her, it seems almost miraculous that Lenna engineered these escapades while she was trapped at home with her nutty family.

"Good for you," she says. "You managed to find some fun."

Lenna gives her a confused look. "Yeah well, it didn't exactly turn out so well."

They pause for a moment to recover from Betsy's misstep and then Lenna continues.

"We usually hooked up at this park—Meadowood. That's where we were, everything the same as usual. The guy, Teddy, even walked me back to my car, and then I got gas across the street, and that's where he was."

Betsy knows this park because it's a stone's throw from the medical center where her dermatologist's office is located. Ball fields and playgrounds surrounded by a paved walking path. She knows the gas station, too, an Exxon with a tiny Circle K that's always hiring. Because of the highway entrance and exit ramps, the area is well lit and usually busy. It's hard to imagine an attack taking place there, though she doesn't doubt it. People, she has learned, do horrible things in plain sight every day.

"He attacked you at the gas station?"

"No. That's just where he took me."

At this point, her story is harder to follow because she keeps interrupting herself and putting events out of order, but the salient details are there: a skinny white man with a scruffy beard and short brown hair. He had a gun and claimed he would shoot her if she didn't hand over the keys. She thought he might be on drugs. There was a woman in a red Circle-K polo behind the window, maybe twenty feet away, but her face was in a magazine the whole time, and when the man grabbed Lenna and pushed her inside her car, she couldn't get the woman's attention. A few cars passed, too, and maybe if she'd yelled, they would have stopped.

"I thought it was a carjacking," she said. "I mean, he was calling me a slut and everything, but I thought he wanted my car, and so I just handed him the keys."

"Okay, well, he had a gun."

"I think he saw me with Teddy," she said. "That's what he acted like—like he'd see me do something bad."

He got Lenna in the car, drove them back across the street to the park and forced her to walk with him to a trail by the creek. She did everything he asked, and then he kicked her in the face.

"That's the part I don't get," she said, her voice cracking a little. "I gave him what he wanted and *then* he beat me up. He must hate women, right?"

Betsy reaches out her hand, and Lenna squeezes it.

Before too long, the SAFE nurse knocks on the door, a tall thin woman with a long gray ponytail and red glasses who has an air of quiet competence.

"Thanks for waiting," she says. "You ready for me?"

Lenna looks alarmed. When Betsy asks if she needs a minute, she says yes.

The door closes and Lenna gives her a shy smile. "So, if I do an exam, and it's not just that asshole's DNA, then what?"

"It's fine," she says. "You'll just have to call the Tinder guy so they can eliminate him."

Lenna's eyes dart across the room and then land on the ceiling. "I don't know him. I wasn't exaggerating. If I saw him during the day, I might not recognize him."

Betsy assures her that she doesn't have to see him or be the one to call, and, although she doesn't make eye contact, Lenna begins to nod.

"I don't mind seeing him. I just don't want to have to tell him what happened."

"Give me his number. I'll call him."

Betsy offers to stay with Lenna for the exam and is relieved when she says no. It's one thing to hear the story of the assault and another to see the fluids glowing under the blacklight, watch the woman's body turn into a crime scene. Back in the hallway, she calls the number Lenna gave her and leaves a message for Teddy to come to the hospital. Then, she zips up her jacket and goes back outside so that she can get some clothes from the collection of SAFE bags she keeps in her trunk now that she has an estimate of Lenna's size. The sky has softened into a deep blue, and she hears the early commuters whipping around the Beltway. She crosses at the walkway and walks to the redbrick parking garage, takes the stairs up to the second floor. Although it's just a little cold, she starts the car so that she can turn on the seat warmers and heat. The exam will take at least thirty minutes and so she allows herself to eat her sandwich and Goldfish crackers, drink some water. Now that she's alone, she feels her fatigue and can sense the beginning of a headache pulsing behind her eyes.

She's worried about Lenna—more so than she usually worries. When she asked if there was someone she could call for support, she had immediately said no, and Betsy had pitied her even though she wouldn't have a good answer herself. Her closest friend, Helen, doesn't drive at night; her friend Margaret has a husband with dementia to care for; and everyone else is the kind of friend she used to have coffee with occasionally. But Lenna is too young to have such little support. When Betsy said she'd have to tell her parents something, she said she would tell them she'd been mugged.

"I *look* like I was mugged; I *feel* like I was mugged," she said proud of herself, it seemed, for outsmarting her parents, "They'll blame me, obviously, but it won't be nearly as bad as if I tell them the truth."

It was hard for her to imagine how these awful conspiracy-believing parents had raised Lenna, but who knew what Andrew's friends— did he have friends these days?—made of Betsy. When she had last seen him, six years ago in Charlotte, she'd been struck by how unhappy, almost dour he seemed. He complained about the traffic, the contractors installing his new custom cabinetry in his kitchen, the religious climate that permeated Southern cities. He had seemed happy only for a brief moment when he'd shown her the new window office at his law firm that he'd earned by making equity partner, and when she had not seemed appropriately impressed by his view of the city's skyline, this had irked him, too.

During her entire visit, he asked her no questions at all about herself. She'd purchased a plane ticket, rented a car, paid for a hotel room, and then she'd barely seen him. There had been the trip to his office followed by one dinner at a bar so loud she couldn't hear him talk and a breakfast at her hotel, most of which he'd spent cursing his phone. When she'd said, very politely—she thought—that his job obviously did not make him happy and that there was more to life than money, he'd told her he'd spent years trying to make her proud of him but that now he was officially giving up.

"I don't know what you're talking about, Andrew," she told him. "I really don't."

"Of course not," he said. "You never do."

Then he gave her a look of total disgust, put on his stylish black overcoat, and left. When she called him, he texted to say they could talk once they'd both cooled down, but they never did. Her messages and calls went unanswered for months and eventually when she called her ex-husband to make sure Andrew was okay, he explained that her son was "taking a break."

"A break *from me*?" she said. "Why?"

He paused for a long time and breathed too loudly into her ear. He was probably pacing. He hated disagreement, hated involving himself in anything that looked like conflict.

"Hello?"

"I don't know what to tell you, Betsy," he said. "You're going to have to work this out with him directly."

About a year after he stopped speaking to her, Andrew transferred to his firm's Los Angeles office—a fact she learned only by googling him—and though he is always on her mind, even more so during the pandemic, she now has no idea where to picture him.

Back in the emergency room, the woman in the burgundy wig has been replaced by an older woman who hasn't heard of a SAFE call and needs to check with someone before she'll buzz her in. When she finally reaches the hallway by the exam room, the door is shut, and the cops are standing beside the counter at the nurse's station.

"Is the nurse still in there?"

The male cop nods. "She's doing a rape kit, thank God. She says we can talk to her afterward."

Betsy's job is simply to support Lenna, and she's a little surprised at how relieved she feels. Intellectually she knows that every case is bad, that every perpetrator has a good chance of being a repeat offender, but the amount of violence toward Lenna seems pathological.

"It's a strong case," the female cop says. "We're going to get this guy and lock him up."

The nurse opens the door looking for fresh clothes, and Betsy hands over the Ziploc bag marked with an S for size small. When the nurse comes out a few minutes later, she's carrying a plastic bag of clothing and the small white box with the black lettering that says SEXUAL ASSAULT EVIDENCE KIT. The cops turn toward the exam room, but the nurse puts up her hand.

"She's asking for the advocate," she says. "She wants to speak to her alone."

Betsy nods at the female cop and then opens the door, holding the weight of it with her palm so it doesn't slam. Lenna is now wearing a baggy pair of gray sweatpants and a long-sleeved T-shirt from the Catholic Charities of Maryland, and her hair has been pulled up into a loop on top of her head. She seems more relaxed, which Betsy realizes is probably just the anxiety meds the nurse gave her kicking in.

"I can't do it," she says. "I changed my mind."

She knows what Lenna means but asks her to clarify.

"I'm not going to report," she says. "I can't."

"Did something happen?"

She shakes her head. "The exam was too much. I just can't."

She sits beside Lenna and touches her arm. "Okay, honey. Let's just sit still for one minute."

They sit for a long stretch without speaking before Betsy goes through all of the options again. She explains that she and the SAFE nurse will be right there when she talks to the police; she tells Lenna that she can stop the questioning at any time. But Lenna doesn't budge.

"I'm sorry," she says, finally, and Betsy knows she has to back off.

"The police are going to think I'm crazy, won't they?"

Lenna is right about the police, but Betsy keeps her face neutral. "They just think you have a strong case. That's all."

Lenna closes her eyes. "I *might* talk to them later," she says. "I just can't do it right now."

"Should I tell them to go?"

She nods.

"Are you sure?" she says. "Do you want to give them any information at all?"

She shakes her head. "I can't."

From the standpoint of the women's shelter, success is measured by how well you advocate for the survivor but sending the police away still feels like a massive failure. Time will be lost, evidence, possibly, will not be collected. Even if Lenna reports tomorrow, the surveillance video at the gas station might already have been deleted.

In the hallway, the police officers seem blindsided.

"We're almost certainly looking at a repeat offender," the female cop says. "If she reports, she can save other women."

"She's been through a lot tonight," Betsy says. "I wouldn't rule it out that she calls you tomorrow."

The female cop shakes her head and turns toward the exam room. "We need to talk now. I'd like to give her one more chance to do the right thing."

The male cop nods. "If it's better with a woman, I'll stay out here."

"The answer is no," Betsy says. "She's not confused. She knows what she's saying."

A flash of anger passes over the female cop's face, and they stare at each other for what feels like a long time.

"This is very unfortunate," the cop finally says. "This guy is just going to rape someone else."

Back in the exam room, Betsy finishes the paperwork while Lenna closes her eyes. After about twenty minutes, the SAFE nurse knocks on the door.

"There's a young man here named Teddy," she says. "He wants to know if he can see you."

Betsy looks to Lenna who shrugs. "Just warn him about my face."

She isn't sure who she was expecting, exactly, but this young man does not seem like the type of person who rendezvouses with near strangers in parking lots. He's probably about Lenna's age, but seems younger—tall and a little chubby with floppy brown hair peeking out of a faded Orioles hat, narrow-ankled sweatpants, plastic slides, long arms, and bad posture. He reminds her of a golden retriever puppy whose feet and limbs are out of proportion to his body.

Lenna adjusts her bed to a higher angle and sits up. "You came."

"Anybody would come," he says. "What happened is so shitty."

"Yep."

Betsy sees him noting her injuries, making a conscious effort not to stare. To his credit, he doesn't ask her to explain anything or force her to deal with his own feelings of guilt. Instead, he thanks her for calling him and pulls a rolling stool over to her bed.

"Here you go," he says and hands her two paper bags from Trader Joes. "I brought you a bunch of random crap from my parents' house."

Lenna opens the first bag and takes out a stack of *Elle* magazines, which he says belong to his sister, a box of assorted party crackers, a bag of Pepperidge Farm cookies, a giant sweatshirt with the name of a local college, a fleece blanket, a first aid kit, which makes them both laugh—"You know I'm in a hospital, right?"—and a board game called Mastermind.

"I'm waiting for stitches, I think," Lenna tells him. "Or something. I don't actually know what I'm waiting for, but I might be here a while."

"I don't care," he says. "I'll stay as long as you want me to."

He digs to the bottom of the bag and pulls out an iPad, begins to list the shows that have been downloaded until she perks up at the name of a sitcom.

"I love *The Office*," she says. "Me getting to watch this right now is the best news I've had all night."

"Good," he says. "Happy to deliver."

Then she turns to Betsy and asks if she needs anything else, which she realizes is a request for her to leave. "You're okay?"

Lenna nods. "I will be."

Teddy adjusts the iPad case into a triangular stand and props it up on the cart hanging over the bed. Lenna scoots to the side of the hospital bed, and pats the space beside her. "Sit here?"

He crawls up beside her and they sit together, not cuddling, but close enough that their arms and bodies touch. They look uncertain but happy.

"Thank you," Lenna says to Betsy. "Seriously, you were a big help. Thanks."

"Call if you need anything," she says, though the number printed on the paperwork is for the women's shelter.

Outside, the soft light of early morning slants down across the parking lot, where the next shift of nurses is beginning to arrive, and her fatigue settles over her body like a shade closing. She could fall asleep right now without trying, but she's not ready to be alone. She takes the slightly longer route past anti-racist Jill's street of stately old homes and towering oaks so that she can go through a Starbucks drive-through for an almond milk latte and then she's back to her neighborhood of row houses and narrow streets lined with closely parked cars. She drives to the playground in the center of the neighborhood, parks her car, and googles Andrew's name, which produces the same results she's seen before—articles in law magazines, his LinkedIn profile, the unsmiling corporate headshot on the law firm's website. His work email is listed right there, and though she suspects he will not appreciate her intrusion into his professional life, she starts an email anyway. *How did it come to this?* is what she wants to say. *Are you never going to speak to me for the rest of my life?* But she knows that what Andrew probably wants from her is an admission of guilt. It would be a small price to pay for him to speak to her again, but she also knows he's wrong. It might comfort him to find a neat explanation for her divorce or Sean's death or the rift between them, but she's old enough to understand the limits of one person's power—to see that the best and worst things that happen in a person's life are never entirely in her control. She can't fully accept the blame for Andrew's feelings about her any more than she can give herself credit for Zaid's.

She takes her coffee to a bench by the small playground, where a young mother pushes a toddler in a baby swing, and watches the porch lights flicker off and the usual joggers and dog walkers begin their morning loops. She doesn't recognize most of these people with their designer exercise outfits and cordless white earbuds, but she has to admit a lot of them are friendly—not just waving at her but sometimes chatting at a distance, too, as if she is a person who they might one day like to know. When she takes out her phone again, she states her position, lets Andrew decide what happens next: *I'm here,* she writes. *If you ever want to be in touch, I'll be ready.*

COMPARE AND CONTRAST

I just read *The Diary of a Young Girl* by Anne Frank, about a girl who hid from the Nazis. There are many similarities but also differences between us: When she started the diary, she was thirteen, and I will be thirteen in August. We are both girls, and like her, I have many secrets and depressed emotions. I never hated my mom the way Anne hated hers, but last spring, I came close.

Anne Frank was born in Germany in 1929, but her family soon moved to the Netherlands, where her dad started a company that manufactured spices and pectin, which is a thickener used in jam. Although she was an immigrant in an unfamiliar place forbidden from going to the movies, leaving her house at night, or doing many other normal things just because she was Jewish, she found ways to be happy. She made many friends, interested many boys, and even charmed her teachers. Then her sister Margot got a notice assigning her to a so-called work camp, and her family moved to a "secret annex" above her dad's warehouse that had rats, cat pee, and no bathtub. They shared the space with another family they didn't especially like and a weird old dentist Anne nicknamed Mr. Idiot.

In contrast, I was born in the United States in 1983 and have always lived in Leechburg, Pennsylvania, a small town known for its stainless steel plants and Mickey Morandini who, as I'm sure you know, plays second base for the Phillies. I have not experienced Anne's hardships, and, unlike her, I do not have a good personality. If I were someone in her journal, I'd probably be Peter. He worries a lot, says little, and admits to being a coward. Anne couldn't believe his postwar plan was to never let on that he was Jewish, but I thought, *That's probably what I'd do in the face of real hardship, too.*

Before I go on, I would like to address the parents who complained about this book's "inappropriate content." I personally think it's good to learn where the cervix is located since I have one and didn't know, and despite what Jessica Hendrick's mom said at the school board meeting, I'm not convinced that the January 6, 1944, entry means Anne was gay. Yes, it does sound gay that she asked to touch her friend Jacque's breasts, and also in the part where she says, "Every time I see a female nude, such as the Venus in my art history book, I go into ecstasy." But Anne also kissed Peter and had crushes on other guys, and when you are just getting used to your new hormones, it's easy for them to misfire and confuse you.

For example, last year in seventh grade we had a new girl named Morgan Vietto who sat in front of me in geometry. She wore long shorts and high-top sneakers, and had the same haircut as Sean Mamros—short in the back with long curtains of hair on top. I actually thought she was a guy—I even thought I had a crush on him—until she turned around to introduce herself. Even after I figured out she was a girl, my body felt light and strange.

Another part I identified with is how hard it is to share close quarters with a man you're not related to, especially if that man is an idiot. In my case, the idiot man is my former stepfather, Wayne, who married my mom when I was in second grade and left three years later when she discovered he was sleeping with his ex-girlfriend. You would think in that time I'd have gotten used to him, but I never did. He had opinions about what I wore, how I spoke to him, and all the extra chores I could be doing. Like Mr. Idiot, he was quick to help himself to treats in our house, like other people's Halloween candy and birthday cupcakes. His back hair and thick yellow toenails appalled me as much as Mr. Idiot's body appalled Anne. When we lived together, he tried to act like he was my father, but as soon as he left, that all stopped. If he sees me through the window when he picks up my twin brothers, he might wave, but that's it. If he takes them to Kennywood or the pool, I'm not invited.

As soon as Wayne moved out, my mom started making me spend time with Uncle Bryan. She said I needed an adult male role model, but I knew she wanted someone to watch me for free, so she could pick up extra shifts at Kmart when Wayne had the twins. Also she was using me to force herself back into my uncle's life. They had been close when they were young, but now, we only saw him at Thanksgiving and Christmas when he appeared at my grandma's house with a pie from Giant Eagle and then left after an hour.

"He always wanted to move away from us," my grandma said about him once. "And now he has."

"Away" was about forty minutes from us in a suburb of Pittsburgh: Instead of farms and homes people couldn't afford to fix, his neighborhood was made up of nearly identical redbrick houses with concrete stoops that overflowed with potted plants. He also had a garage, and this was where we spent a lot of our time.

Uncle Bryan never had any kid activities planned. It was more like, "Hey, let's go to AutoZone and then give this truck an oil change." Or, "Anybody ever teach you how to use a miter saw?" He didn't say much except to explain what we were doing, but he liked that I wanted to know how things worked, and he trusted me with his tools, which his roommate, Gary, told me is a sign of real affection. He also made delicious egg salad sandwiches with bacon and showed me how to use his grill. The secret is using your meat thermometer. Just like Anne Frank eventually came to appreciate Peter, I came to appreciate Bryan.

Another similarity between me and Anne is that we lived in the shadow of big secrets. Her secret was being alive in a place where Jewish people were forced to flee or suffer. My secret was actually my uncle's secret.

One Saturday, instead of taking me to his house, my mom drove us to a hiking trail by the Kiski River and said my uncle had gotten some very bad news and was going to need his Saturdays free to deal with it. I was eleven and surely old enough to stay home alone, wasn't I?

"I don't get it," I said.

It was November, cold enough to see our breath in the air. We had gotten out of the car and she was making this big deal out of retying her tennis shoes. I got the feeling she didn't want to make eye contact.

"What?" I said. "What did I do?"

"What are you talking about? You didn't do anything. Bryan's sick."

When I asked if it was cancer, she sobbed and wiped at her nose with a wad of Kleenex. We took the yellow footbridge that always swings so fast it makes you sick, and then followed a muddy path along the river. Leaves were all over the trail. After about twenty minutes we got to a big outcropping of rocks on the riverbank, where we stopped to eat the blueberry freezer bagels she'd brought in her purse.

"If he's sick, though, maybe I should go over there and help."

My mom was wearing a striped Colors of Benetton stocking cap from the lost and found at Kmart. When she shook her head no, the puff ball on its top wobbled. "It's not that kind of sick," she said, a mouthful of bagel in her cheek.

I thunked a rock into the water, followed by another. Eventually, my mom asked if I could keep a secret. I told her okay. "Kayla Marie, I'm serious," she said. "I mean from everyone, including Heather."

Heather Slifko was my best friend and I had told her many secret things, such as the fact that my bio-dad was some old married guy my mom had slept with as a teenager who literally paid her to stay out of his life, and about the night my mom had dragged me and my brothers out of bed to see if she could spot Wayne's truck at his ex-girlfriend's house, and how when we found Wayne's truck, she took out a bar of Dove soap she'd packed for this very purpose and drew a giant penis on his windshield with an arrow and the word *YOU*.

"If you tell someone, Bryan could lose his job," she said. "Are you ready for that kind of responsibility?"

At this point I got it—how many diseases are such a big secret?—but I still hoped I was wrong. Once, Wayne had pointed out a man on the sidewalk who had big reddish-purple spots blooming on his face. Wayne said the spots meant AIDS, and I pressed my face against the minivan window and didn't even try to pretend I wasn't staring. Knowing AIDS was just feet away felt like the most terrible and exciting thing that had ever happened to me. I couldn't imagine it would come closer.

"Just tell me."

There were another five minutes of warnings before she spit it out.

Obviously, Anne's secret was much bigger than mine but a similarity is how our secrets always stayed at the back of our minds. Anne worried an open window or flushed toilet would get them murdered, and I thought about how AIDS would kill my uncle. After my mom stopped taking me to Bryan's, I spent my Saturdays watching cartoons or sitting in Heather's bedroom, hearing how great it was we were in junior high with eighth-grade boys like Danny Piekarski who'd once held her hand on the bus. In elementary school, neither of us had been popular, but now that she had made the middle-school cheer team, her status was changing.

The power of my secret became nearly irresistible whenever I thought about the reaction I'd get to see on Heather's face, but then, my mother's voice in my head warned me to keep my mouth shut and not ruin Bryan's life. This turned out to be lucky because a few months later Heather found a fleet of LEGO starships I was building in the basement and decided I was too uncool to be her friend.

At first it was a relief not to see Bryan because I didn't know any-thing about HIV and was scared I would get it and give it to my little brothers, but I also worried about him and I couldn't understand how my mother could cut him out of our lives.

"Don't be so dramatic," my mom said. "That's not what's happening. He has a lot to deal with right now, and we're giving him some space."

She was at the stove cooking "rice, peas, and cheese," a made-up dish we used to eat only when she was very tired—the entire recipe was melting those ingredients together. Ever since Wayne left, we ate it at least once a week. My brothers were in the living room playing Nin-tendo, close enough that I couldn't talk freely.

"Okay."

"Has it occurred to you that he doesn't want to see us?"

I tried not to let on how much this hurt my feelings, but my mom seemed to know, and she pulled me against her into a side hug while she stirred dinner. "He's dealing with some heavy stuff right now, honey," she said. "Don't take it personally."

\ \ \ \ \ \ \

The next time my mom was at work I found Bryan's name in her address book and sent him a long letter about how I'd enjoyed getting to know him and that because of his technical instruction I was start-ing to think I might try to be an engineer. I said I knew he probably wanted to spend his remaining days with Gary but that it was still very sad to think I'd never see him again.

The following Saturday he called to tell me that, as far as he knew, his death was not imminent and the chances of me seeing him again were extremely good. "I'm very sorry nobody explained this to you, Kayla," he said. "I hope we can see each other again soon."

"Mom said you want some space."

He sighed. In the background I could hear the vacuum cleaner, and Alan Jackson singing about living his "honky-tonk dream."

"You're welcome here whenever your mom says it's okay."

I asked if I would see him at my grandma's for Christmas dinner—he had skipped Thanksgiving—and he said probably not because she had asked him not to bring Gary now that the cat was out of the bag on them being boyfriends.

"Oh."

"Yeah, I can't do that to him." He explained that Gary, who was not HIV positive, was a kind person and that it was foolish of my grandmother to assume that just because he was twelve years older he had been the one to "recruit Bryan to his lifestyle."

"She needs to blame someone," he said. "She can't believe this is who I am."

This was the most he had ever told me about his personal life and although I wanted him to keep talking, I wasn't sure what to say. I had never met a gay person before. "Well," I said, "I'll work on my mom."

That night, when I told my mom what Bryan had said, she admitted she was mad at him. "He lied to me about himself for a very long time, Kayla. I don't even know who he is anymore."

My brothers were at Wayne's house, and we were on the couch watching *Wheel of Fortune* and eating a frozen pizza she'd bought from a fire department fundraiser. I didn't want to start a fight, but I knew that if I didn't say something, I might never see Uncle Bryan again.

"Okay," I said. "So, we should get to know him."

My mom shook her head. "When you're an adult, you'll understand why he's not a good role model for you."

"Yes he is," I said. "All we do is use tools and fix things. He said he'll help me with my science fair project."

My mom sighed. On TV, a man with a handlebar mustache named Jerry solved the puzzle and won a trip to Alaska. "I've been trying to protect you from all of this, Kayla," she said. "Do you think I want to have to tell you about your uncle's sex life?"

The blood rushed to my face, and I couldn't look at her, which was probably the point.

"He didn't get this from Gary, you know," she said. "He got it from a stranger. Do you think a person who goes to sex parties is a good role model?"

I picked up my brother's Teenage Mutant Ninja Turtle action figure and spun its plastic arm around.

"He's not who you think he is," she said.

Bryan didn't come to Christmas. When I asked my mom to see him over winter break, she said maybe, and then that she was busy, and at some point, I stopped asking, and then it was time to go back to school.

\ \ \ \ \ \ \

When I say Anne Frank had a good personality, I mean she was optimistic and happy. When she got a report card with a D, a C-, and zero As, she said, "My report card wasn't too bad." When she thought about spending her adolescence in hiding, she decided it was a good beginning for an interesting life. When people criticized her, she didn't like it, but she didn't let their opinions hurt her self-confidence. In contrast, my natural instinct is pessimism. When someone doesn't like me, I feel ashamed.

With Heather, I'd known something was going on for a while, but I didn't realize how bad things were until I tried to sit with her at lunch that first day back in January, and she said her table was full.

"No it's not," I said. "There's plenty of space."

She said she was saving those spots.

When I didn't move right away, Heather's friend Cindy—the least popular and, therefore, meanest of her new friends—told me to go away. "Our table is full today and tomorrow and forever," she said. "There isn't ever going to be space for you."

I'm sure I was standing there with my lunch tray for less than a minute, but it felt much longer. I was trying to find a place to sit without drawing more attention when I saw Morgan Vietto sitting with two girls I didn't recognize. When she saw me, she gave me such a welcoming grin my adrenaline transformed into euphoria.

"Kayla," she said. "You know Lisa and Amy, right?"

The two plain, soft-spoken girls introduced themselves, and Morgan explained they'd met last summer at basketball camp. Unlike Heather and the cheerleaders, there seemed to be no threat of being made fun of, and I soon felt relaxed and let my mind wander to my science fair project about circuits, and if I'd still be able to do it without Bryan's help. When Morgan asked if I would join them for basketball tryouts the following week, I had to ask her to repeat the question.

"Oh, no. Probably not," I said. "I don't know how to play."

Morgan was close enough that I could see two empty earring holes in each ear, and a spray of gold flecks circling the pupils in her hazel eyes. There was something boyish about the way she carried herself.

"You should," Amy said. "You're tall and you run fast in gym class."

I said I'd think about it, and this was enough to get me invited to the YMCA with Morgan and her older brother that Saturday so she could teach me the basics.

"Do you like basketball?" my mom asked in the minivan on the way over. "I wasn't aware you played sports voluntarily."

Her hesitance, I knew, was about the twins who I often watched after school, and who would have to start going to my grandma's house if I had practice to go to. But I also knew if I said it was important to me, she would let me try out for the team. "I like running," I said. "I like chasing people. It's pretty much the same thing."

"Well, I'm glad you're making new friends."

This was a dig at Heather who had offended her years ago by pointing out a hairline crack in our nicest serving bowl, so I rolled my eyes.

"Calm down. I'm not criticizing anyone," she said. "I just think it's great you're meeting new people."

/ / / / / / /

The YMCA was a cinder-block building with a large Y made of glass blocks. While Morgan's dad and brother lifted weights, we went to the gym, where Morgan showed me how to pass the ball with two hands and shoot with one. She told me about traveling and double dribbling and rebounded for me while I practiced hurling the ball at the hoop. After about an hour of airballs, a group of teenage boys showed up and asked if Morgan wanted to play in their pickup game.

"Go ahead," I said. "I'll watch."

"You can play, too," one of the guys said. "We'll do full court four on four and use a sub. We play to fifteen but you have to win by two."

I did not want to play but said sure.

I understood from how often Morgan got the ball that she had earned the respect of these older guys in previous games. She was quick and made most of her shots and could predict where the rebound would go. The one time I got the ball, I bounced it twice and returned it. As soon as the guy who'd stepped out returned from the water fountain, I let him back in. Midway through the second game, Morgan's dad appeared and asked in a sort of jokey voice if I was getting to play, too, or if Morgan was just making me watch her have fun.

"It's okay. I like to watch her," I said, and then, seeing the confusion on his face, added, "I'm still learning."

Basketball tryouts involved more running than shooting and wouldn't you know, I made the team. After that, I saw Morgan every day at lunch and basketball practice and sometimes at her house on the weekends. By the end of February, she had taken up the empty space left by Heather, but our friendship was completely different. We didn't share secrets and give each other makeovers. Hanging out with Morgan was more like hanging out with Bryan. Nothing we did felt like anything that should be especially fun to me—skateboarding, watching NBA games she'd recorded, playing *Duck Hunt* on her Nintendo—but I liked being in the same place as Morgan. I had a crush on her. What I didn't know was if it was a real crush or if the person I liked was the imaginary boy I'd mistaken her for when we'd first met.

One night I asked my mom how you knew if you had a crush on someone.

"Why?" she said. "Who is it?"

"Never mind."

I was finishing my lab report at the dining-room table, and she was on the couch, flipping through a magazine.

"You feel funny around them," she said finally. "That's about it. That and I guess you know where they are in a room without checking."

I decided to test this know-where-they-are theory the next day at basketball practice since I'd already failed the feeling-funny-around-them test.

"So?" She was raising her eyebrows and staring at me, and I said it was Billy Schaffer, who I knew was nice enough not to make fun of me if my mom acted weird around him.

"It's hopeless, anyway," I said. "He's already dating someone."

"That's too bad," she said, but I could tell she was happy I was telling her my secrets.

The next day at breakfast my mom said she'd changed her mind, and if I still wanted to spend my school's Vocational Day with Bryan, it was fine. She was being too nice about it, and I had the sick feeling that she knew I had a crush on Morgan and was giving me a chance to discuss it with a gay person.

"I don't understand," I said. "What happened?"

"Don't you want to go anymore?"

I shrugged.

"I thought you'd be happy," she said. "I feel like I can't win with you."

Two weeks later Bryan pulled up in his work van before the sun had fully risen, hopped out with the engine running, and handed me a gas station donut. I'd expected him to look skinny or sick but he looked the same—a twenty-something brown-haired man with broad shoulders and small eyes who looked a lot like my mother. I was nervous about the hours I'd have to spend trying not to say the wrong thing.

"Be good," my mom called after me, and then, as if it was an afterthought, "Have fun."

There was still snow on the ground, and the van was stuffy and warm from the heater, which was on its highest setting.

"I crank it way up," Bryan said, following my gaze. "You let me know if you get hot."

There was a layer of dirt and gravel everywhere, faint muddy footprints on the floor mats streaked with melted road salt. Below my feet, which didn't quite reach the floor, were a roll of shop towels, a wide plastic thermos, and a red and white cooler. "And that stuff, too," he said. "I can move it."

"I'm good," I said. "Thanks for letting me follow you around."

He grinned. "Guess where we're going?"

I knew he worked in hospitals, banks, hotels, rich people's boats—basically anywhere that anyone might have a generator. But I didn't have a guess as to what place would make him this happy.

"I don't know. I give up."

"Spring Fling out in Westmoreland County," he said. "It's like a carnival with rides."

"Cool."

"Right?" he said. "Couldn't have planned it better if I tried."

Bryan said he'd be doing maintenance and repair on a generator that wasn't working, and I nodded along, feeling guilty that he was being nice to me after my family had abandoned him. I hadn't seen him in months, hadn't spoken to him since that one phone call, and he acted like nothing was wrong.

I watched the bare trees flicker past and wondered if I should bring up his disease, but he ended up saying something first. "Listen," he said, "you've been told some heavy stuff about me, and I want you to know you can ask questions."

There were a million questions: How did he get it? Was he scared? Did he hate our family? Was he going to die soon? Was what my mom said about the sex parties true? But almost nothing that seemed appropriate to ask. "Do you feel sick all the time?" I asked instead.

He smiled and shook his head no. He explained that other than the flu-like symptoms that had made him get tested in the first place, he felt the same, and that when he did get symptoms, it would mean his HIV had become AIDS.

"Right," I said and felt myself blush. Other than the *Junior Scholastic* articles I'd read in Civics about Ryan White and a lady who'd gotten HIV from her ungloved dentist, I didn't know anything about HIV.

"Don't look so worried," Bryan said. "For now, I'm okay."

/ / / / / / /

At first it was just us and a handful of janitors at the fairgrounds and then, slowly, the concession stand windows opened and the air filled with the smells of fried oil and sugar. Rows of plastic canopy tents covered the asphalt. In the daylight, the dinginess of the rides was obvious. When the Spring Fling opened to the public at ten, the space still felt ordinary and empty, nothing like the fairs I'd gone to at night when most of the fun was the crowd and the darkness itself, the sense that you were in a strange world where anything could happen.

My disappointment was overshadowed by the excitement of going behind the scenes with an expert. Bryan showed me how to inspect coolant lines and drive belts, how to check for oil leaks. We replaced air filters, removed water from the fuel tanks.

We ate lunch at a picnic table overlooking a field edged by brown, leafless trees. For the special occasion, my mom had packed me a Lunchable, and I ate each cracker and cheese slice individually so it would last longer. About twenty feet away from us, a girl with ripped jeans and frosted hair leaned against the chain-link fence and made out with a guy in a Steelers hat whose jeans were so loose they showed his boxers—the kind of sloppy tongue-kissing that would make a hall monitor spray us with a squirt bottle if we tried it at school.

When Bryan saw me staring, he laughed. "Young love," he said. "Good for them. Soon enough that'll be you."

I shook my head. I knew I seemed like every other girl who can't imagine she'll ever do the "gross" things adults do, but what if I was different and this grossed-out feeling never went away?

"You don't like anyone yet?"

I shrugged. I wondered if his new chattiness had to do with his illness, or if what I had thought of as his reserved personality was just him being in the closet.

"Did you like someone at this age? Did you even . . ."

"Know I was gay?"

I nodded.

"Yes," he said. "Ben Miller."

Ben Miller was his friend from Cub Scouts, and he'd been tortured by a secret love of him for years. To this day, he was pretty sure his friend had no idea. When I asked how he'd known he was gay, he squinted at me as if he finally saw me, and I felt my whole body turn hot.

"I don't know," he said. "For me at least, it wasn't ever a big mystery."

After lunch we finished the maintenance and organized the back of his work van. One generator needed a part he'd have to bring back the next day. On our way out he stopped at a cinder-block building to talk to the manager, and she handed him a roll of red tickets. "Take her on some rides," she said. "Stay as long as you like."

Bryan made me call my mom from a payphone and with her permission, we stayed until dusk, riding every ride we could until the tickets ran out.

\ \ \ \ \ \ \

I had thought that after Vocational Day, I'd start going back to Bryan's house, but my mom always said it was too far or a bad time, and then by summer he was very sick. Every few weeks, Gary would call from the hospital to tell my mom Bryan was dehydrated or had low sodium or pneumonia or some new problem I didn't understand.

Depending on which nurse was on duty, Gary wasn't allowed in his room, so my mom would drive down there so someone could be with him.

Usually my mom went by herself while I watched my brothers. The one time I got to go, Bryan was half asleep with an oxygen tube in his nose that kept coming unhooked. He was so out of it he didn't notice his hospital gown was open and showing his underwear. His face was so skinny it looked like it had a completely different shape. A blood pressure cuff beside his bed was labeled SMALL ADULT.

When he saw me, he smiled and made this clicking noise with his mouth. "I'm sorry about the science fair project, Kayla," he said. "I was looking forward to that."

I told him it was okay, but he seemed loopy and I'm not sure he heard.

Every time Bryan went to the hospital, I was convinced it was the end. But for a long time, it wasn't, and the terror of those false alarms made me think of Bryan while reading Anne Frank's diary. She lived with the sounds of machine-gun fire and air sirens and bombings, and I'm sure she was frightened all the time. My classmates thought her family should have listened to the warnings and relocated, but how can you save yourself when there's nowhere else to go?

Bryan died at home with Gary, having what they had thought was a good day. He went to sleep and didn't wake up. This was four months ago, ten days before Christmas, and almost exactly one year since we found out he was sick. He'd just had a big fight with my mom and I was mad at him, too, because he'd apparently suggested to my mom that I was gay and that her homophobic attitude was bad for me.

"Did you tell him something like that Kayla?" my mom asked. "If you did, you're not in trouble, but I need to know."

My brothers were asleep, but I was still up reading. I couldn't speak at first, and so I shook my head, pretended I was too tired to focus.

"Did something happen with Heather?" she said. "Is that why—"

"Nothing happened!" I said. "He's just making it up."

"Okay."

"He's probably trying to hurt you. I didn't say anything."

She stayed there on the edge of my bed, rubbing my back. Her eyes were smudged with old makeup. "He said a lot of other mean things, too," she said. "I know he's angry, but I wish he wouldn't take it out on me."

"I know."

"It's not like I did this to him. And I didn't abandon him like a lot of people would have, either. If he wants to blame someone, he should blame himself."

The next day I called to ask Bryan what he'd been thinking, but Gary answered the phone and I just let him say, "Hello? Hello? Hello?"

As for Morgan, in case you're wondering, nothing happened between us, and then at the end of the school year she moved back to her mom's house in Kittanning, where the school's basketball team is a lot better. I haven't heard much from her even though it's just twenty minutes away, but I still consider her to be what Anne called a "true friend." When Bryan died, I called Morgan crying, and she made her brother come get me. It was freezing outside, but she asked if I wanted to play basketball in her driveway, which I realized was what would have made her feel better in this situation, so I said yes. While I dribbled, her body hovered behind me like a shadow. When we stopped for a break, I said I was supposed to say my uncle died of cancer but that it wasn't the truth. Then I told her he was gay. "I'm supposed to keep this a secret, but I don't want to," I said. "I want someone to know."

She hugged me and then suggested we switch from one-on-one to H-O-R-S-E, which was my favorite basketball-related game. She didn't say much else about Bryan except to ask what he was like. I said he liked country music and bacon and that he'd taught me about tools and machines.

She seemed to think that was cool. Then she said, "I don't care about people being gay. I think it's fine."

I looked for a sign that this was some kind of confession or invitation, but her expression told me nothing.

"I think it's fine, too," I said, by which I meant, "It's okay if you kiss me; it doesn't have to mean anything." But she didn't.

As I'm sure you've noticed, there are many similarities between Bryan and Anne—the hiding and secrets, the fact they both had unchangeable things about themselves that made other people wish they were dead—but I didn't tell you about Bryan to compare him with Anne. I wanted to explain something else about me. Several times Anne talks about how guilty she feels to be alive when others weren't. She felt she'd abandoned her childhood friend Hanneli. "Oh Anne, why have you deserted me?" Hanneli asks in a dream, and Anne wishes for a time when she'll be able to look into her friend's face and apologize, even though she didn't actually do anything wrong. The difference is that I did stop calling and visiting Bryan. I also told my mom he was a liar, and even though I knew how it felt, I acted like I wanted him to go away.

At the Spring Fling, we had saved the scariest roller coaster for last—it started with a steep hill and then immediately flipped us upside down with a sudden jerk. People screamed and squealed in delight, but Bryan, who had seen the flimsiness of the ride, seemed genuinely scared. "Oh my God, listen to that, Kayla," he'd said as it squeaked and clattered. "Jesus." At the next swerve, he reached for my hand but I panicked and pulled away, tried to pretend I was fixing my ponytail. He didn't say anything and acted normal the whole way home, but he knew I had rejected him.

Sometimes when I can't sleep, I replay this scene in my mind. When I get depressed, I tell myself that what Anne said about herself is true of me, too: I am mostly good. In spite of my many faults, I am a person who is capable of change.

FAMILY
RESEMBLANCE

Every summer we met up in a different city where one of our families lived. San Diego, Minneapolis, Camden, Pittsburgh. Other than a brief excursion to a butterfly garden or beach, every trip was essentially the same—hotel breakfasts with stainless steel coffee dispensers and plastic canisters of Cheerios and Froot Loops, hours in a dimly lit hotel pool where the kids splashed around and the adults drank the gin and tonics or vodka sours we'd poured into insulated coffee mugs in our hotel rooms. We knew the faint outlines of everyone's separate lives back home in their distant cities or suburbs, but these trips were for our children, and every conversation centered on them and "Jake Gyllenhaal"—the sensitive skin, the aptitude for spatial relationships, those big blue eyes and thick brown hair. To see all of them in one place made us dizzy.

That first summer, there had been eleven families who'd signed up for the sibling registry. By the second summer, there had been sixteen, and every summer after that, a slow trickle that added up to a number that was beginning to make us uneasy. When would the vials finally run out? When would children who looked like our children stop being born? And, considering that we had yet to meet one of those hetero, two-parent families who grinned at us from the website—we were lesbian couples and Alex, a single mother by choice from the Detroit suburbs—how many other families were out there? But as anxious as some of us were, we were also grateful to be living in this moment and in this country, to have the thousands of dollars needed to create our families—and we were grateful for this group, which would provide our children with a glimpse into the other half of their DNA, a chance, perhaps, to make up a little of what had been lost in being born this way. And so, when a new family arrived, we answered the questions we always answered about our children's health, second parent adoption, the best phrases and phases to explain all of this to a child. We cooed over their babies and welcomed these new people into our fold.

The eighth summer, there was just one new family—Izzy and Olivia and their nine-month-old daughter, Hattie. We knew already from our Facebook group that they were cooler and more attractive than the rest of us, but we didn't fully appreciate just how beautiful they were until we saw them in person. Izzy was slim and delicate with chin-length platinum hair, sharp cheekbones, blue eyes edged with dark liner. Many of us had never been women who felt comfortable in high heels or lipstick and now that we were parents approaching middle age, we dressed entirely for utility and comfort—cargo shorts and Fruit of the Loom T-shirts, Teva sandals we'd owned since before our children were born. Izzy wore leather flats and a silk blouse tucked into a pair of stiff high-waisted denim pants we understood must be trendy. She had the small, lithe body of a dancer and movements so graceful she made us self-conscious about how we carried our bodies.

Of the two of them, Izzy was the more conventionally attractive—she looked like a model—but it was Olivia, with her short edgy haircut and her masculine energy, who especially intrigued us. She was alluring in the androgynous, macho way that felt both familiar and also completely reimagined—a better, sexier version of ourselves. Tall and lean, wearing long cutoffs and skateboarding sneakers, a faded T-shirt from an indie rock band we didn't know, the magnetic pull of a stylish tomboy old enough to have harnessed her powers. When she introduced herself, her handshake was firm and she held our gaze just long enough to make our hearts beat a little faster.

"Call me Liv," she said, her voice low and husky as if she had just woken up. "It's good to finally meet all of you."

A group of us had just arrived at the rental car counters at the El Paso airport, and the kids were all tired of traveling and sticky with the milk and graham crackers we'd given them on the plane. Hattie was strapped into a tiny blue ergonomic stroller, half asleep, her pale cheeks flushed pink, her wispy baby hair slightly damp. She had Liv's brown eyes and Jake Gyllenhaal's thick eyelashes and thin pink lips. Like the rest of us, Izzy and Liv were carrying bags and a car seat, but all of their belongings seemed better designed and more compact than our own.

"Cool stroller," Jenna, a mother from Milwaukee, said. "It's tiny but looks so sturdy."

Liv shrugged. "It's from some European company, but we got it from a neighbor for fifteen bucks. The tot swap scene in Brooklyn is crazy."

Our hosts, Amanda and Beth, lived an hour away in Las Cruces, and we had already sorted out ahead of time who would share car rentals, but now that we were in person, it was hard not to want to renegotiate. Was everyone happy in their assigned cars? Did anyone want to grab a spot in one of the minivans we'd rented? We did not ask why it was that Alex and her mother, two straight people who could never fully appreciate this couple or their magnetism, deserved this first hour of uninterrupted access to them, so instead we simply stood at the bottom of the escalator with jealousy, watching them disappear into the dark of the parking garage.

We'd booked rooms at a Hampton Inn Suites just off the highway, nestled in a crowded strip of hotels and chain steak houses, whose main attraction was a rickety yellow waterslide at the edge of the indoor pool. It was July and hot. From our balconies we could see the flat brown desert dotted with green patches of yucca and beargrass, the jagged gray edge of the Organ Mountains rising in the distance, and we could feel the dry heat encircling us. We took showers, styled our hair, put on our newest and most flattering clothing, and then we drove to the Mexican restaurant, a large white adobe building decorated with paper lanterns and strings of dried chilis, that Amanda and Beth promised had the best margaritas and green enchiladas.

Seventeen families had made the trip this year, and the staff had set us up in our own private space—two long tables in a narrow room with mustard yellow walls and a decorative adobe oven inside of which someone had taped orange cardboard flames. We all rushed to choose the closest spots as possible to Izzy and Liv and strained to hear what they had to say over the swell of conversation and the screams of children. The only people who could fully participate in their conversations were sitting directly beside them, but this didn't stop the rest of us from trying. Already, there was a desperate, self-effacing feeling in the air. It was embarrassing, we were adults—pharmacists, nurses, software engineers, firefighters—but now we had become teenagers who wanted our proximity to the cool kids to transform us.

Soon black plastic bowls of chips and salsa arrived along with the rest of our group, and those of us who were not breastfeeding ordered our first round of margaritas, which came in flavors like blackberry habanero and prickly pear. As soon as the alcohol hit our bloodstream, our nerves calmed enough that we focused on the people directly across from us and on our children who wanted to pound the table or play with sugar packets or chase each other down the hallways of the bustling restaurant. We opened our menus and became absorbed with our choices.

A team of two waitresses took down all of our orders and then, through the echoes of conversation, we heard Stacey squeal, "Oh my God, that's amazing!" and say the name of a relatively famous African American actress.

"It's been a good year," Liv said. "I've been working on smaller projects for decades, but I finally feel like this film could have legs."

The film was a futuristic sci-fi story about two American families—one Black and one white—who were both vacationing in Sweden when an asteroid destroyed most of the earth. Ill-equipped to survive the resulting battle for resources in this foreign country, the families worked together to commandeer a reindeer farm, confronting their stereotypes in the process.

"It sounds cheesier than I think it is," she said. "I guess we'll see."

Izzy touched Liv's hand across the table before looking back at Stacey. "It's good," she said. "*She's* good."

Liv smiled at Izzy and squeezed her hand. It was obvious that they were not just in love but still entranced with each other, and this was another thing to envy—that current of passion between them that had somehow managed to survive all the sleepless nights and diaper changes.

"Izzy's in the film industry, too," Liv said. "She does set design."

We quickly gathered that Izzy, who was nearly a decade younger than Liv and whose most famous gig seemed to be a discontinued Hulu show none of us had heard of, was not especially established, and so we asked just enough questions to be polite. Then we turned back to Liv. We wanted to know about celebrities and film locations, and we also wanted to know what exactly it was that a cinematographer did.

"Maybe this is the wrong way to say it," Lindsay said. "But do you have a particular aesthetic you go for?"

Lindsay was a tall, stern-looking cat veterinarian with short iron gray hair and two kids who had been birthed by her friendlier wife, Stacey, a Vietnamese American artist who sold watercolors of sunsets and beach scenes from her Etsy shop. Apparently, they both volunteered each year at a horror film festival in New Orleans and had many thoughts about low-budget horror films they had already shared with Liv.

"I do what the filmmaker wants," Liv said. "But I like natural light and realism. I hate it when something is so touched up in post-production that it looks fake."

She gave examples of films she thought were overproduced and films she admired. In one of her favorite movies, the stills all looked like old master oil paintings; in another, each cut transitioned seamlessly to the next with a subtle visual echo. Although most of us didn't know what she was talking about, we understood that we were in the presence of a professional, and also, perhaps, on some level, that she was showing us a different, better way of seeing. When most of us watched movies, we did not think about light and shadow or how the width of a shot altered the emotion of a scene, but now, maybe, we would.

For the rest of the weekend, a feeling of excitement rippled through the group that was less about Izzy and Liv and more about a new feeling of possibility that we had for our own lives. Around them, we felt inspired to dress up and have more interesting conversations, to reach for each other's bodies at night once our kids were tucked into the pack-n-plays and air mattresses behind the French doors of our hotel rooms. It was amazing to us that these sophisticated women had made the same choices that we had made to produce a child who was related to our children, and maybe, it meant something. Maybe in some small way, we were the same as they were, and, therefore, better than we had thought. For many of us, these gatherings were a duty not unlike soccer games or PTA meetings: We participated largely because this group might someday matter to our children. We gave ourselves permission to skip summers and our relationships with each other were always something shy of real friendships. That year though, when we waved goodbye at the airport a feeling of genuine sadness hung in the air.

/ / / / / / /

Over the next year, we watched Liv's movies and followed the interviews she gave in film magazines about the sci-fi movie, which was not widely released but had won an award at a film festival and given her career new momentum. When you searched her name, there were three new films she'd signed on to, all with at least one actor we recognized. We educated ourselves enough to have informed conversations about film the following summer in Milwaukee, but then, two weeks before the trip was scheduled, she posted in the Facebook group that they wouldn't be able to come after all. Izzy was trying to get pregnant and her IUI was likely going to be right in the middle of our long weekend.

We're bummed to miss it, she wrote. *Have a drink for us in the hotel pool and see you next year!*

Without them, Milwaukee was less charged than we'd hoped but still elevated by their presence in our conversations and by the itinerary we'd planned in an effort to impress them. We went to the art museum, ate tofu tacos and Indonesian rice from food trucks. In the hotel pool, woozy from Manhattans and Aperol spritzes, we admitted just how much time we'd spent googling these women over the past twelve months, how electrifying it was to be in their presence. It was not about their celebrity, we decided, or not *just* about that—it was that they were both trained to see and create beauty, that they inspired us to find more beauty too. Around them, we expected more from our lives, believed we were still young enough for something new and surprising to happen to us.

"They're just people," said McCray, a firefighter from Jacksonville. "I don't think we need to lose our shit about it."

Those of us with kids old enough to swim by themselves were sitting on the side of the pool, out of earshot of the children, but McCray's wife, Chelsea, still winced at the word "shit."

"Okay, sorry," McCray said. "But you know what I mean. Just because they're all Hollywood or whatever doesn't mean their you-know-what doesn't stink."

McCray was an army veteran who was built like a cinder block with a bleach-blond buzzcut and a series of unfortunate tattoos—a dagger on her thigh, Super Mario on her forearm—and she could not be relied upon to understand the unspoken rules of our mostly middle-class group. She used "fart" instead of "toot," unselfconsciously drank PBR and Bud Light, and had gotten into a heated conversation with Celia and Lee a couple of summers ago after she'd used "dad" instead of "donor."

"I hear you, McCray," Alex said. "We've been getting a little obsessed."

We all liked Alex, an easygoing hospital administrator in her forties who never seemed uncomfortable being the only straight or single person in the group, and as soon as she spoke, McCray seemed to relax.

"Right?" she said. "They're just people. Being famous doesn't make you magic."

We paused long enough to allow McCray to think she had made her point with us, and then, as soon as she left to help her kid inflate his raft, our conversation went back to Izzy and Liv. Yes, they were just people, but also, they were different than anyone we'd ever met, different than anyone we would have had any hopes of meeting if we had not been forced to make our families in this strange and sometimes terrifying way and wasn't that the silver lining here—these random, beautiful connections that had made the world seem bigger and smaller at the same time?

/ / / / / / /

We had all started to follow them on Instagram and Twitter, and saw that Izzy did not get pregnant that summer—and, from the handful of short exchanges we saw in the Facebook group, her fertility seemed to be an ongoing and stressful project for both her and Liv who, at thirty-nine was likely too old to get pregnant again. Other than that, though, their lives seemed to be better than ever. They bought a tiny brownstone in Park Slope and the photographs looked like something you'd see in a magazine—wool rugs, original artwork, pots of bright green houseplants in the corners. Liv signed on to an action movie that was being made by an Oscar-nominated director and was also directing her first film, an indie drama about a back-to-the-land commune in Arkansas. Izzy's feed was filled with vegan pies and cupcakes and antique furniture she'd found and refurbished. There was also a viral video of Hattie, bundled up in a snowsuit, looking up at falling snow and asking it to stop—"Not today snow! I'm playing!"—which even those who did not approve of putting their kids on social media had to admit was cute. We were happy for their good fortune, which felt, in a way, like our good fortune, and when we saw them the following summer, we were shocked to learn that they were in couples counseling.

"It's been a hard year," Izzy told us that first night, after the kids had gone to sleep. "But we're trying to work it out."

We were outside, sitting around a sandy firepit, about thirty feet from a lake house we'd rented in a small Michigan town on the coast of Lake Huron, about three hours northeast of Alex's house in Plymouth. The lake house, which had two floors of small bedrooms with adjoining bathrooms as well as a yoga room large enough for three air mattresses, belonged to Alex's parents who ran yoga retreats and mediation seminars. Some of our group was going to stay in the house for a whole week—Sunday through Sunday—and the rest would join us for the weekend and stay in area hotels. It could have been the intimacy of this small group that made Izzy so forthcoming, but we also got the feeling that she was lonely and needed to talk. Liv was inside at the dining-room table, illuminated behind the sliding glass doors, working on her laptop, finishing up what she promised would be her last work for the week.

"I wanted another baby," Izzy said. "When it didn't happen, I was devastated and pissed off at Liv who didn't seem to care."

Since we'd last seen her, she'd let her hair return to its natural dishwater blond, and, although she was still beautiful, this new hair color combined with her lack of makeup made her seem more approachable.

"That sucks," McCray said. "That really sucks."

"Are you still trying?" Alex asked. "I mean, if that's not too personal to ask."

Izzy shook her head and picked up her feet. She was seated on a weathered wooden swing along with McCray and Chelsea, and the rest of us were in plastic deck chairs.

"I can't," she said. "Or, I guess I don't want to anymore. They're out of vials."

"Oh, Izzy," Alex said. "I'm so sorry it didn't work."

"I did get pregnant. Twice, actually, but I had miscarriages."

The miscarriages had been sad, of course, but also expensive. Each D&C had cost nearly a grand and because her insurance only covered fertility treatments for same-sex couples after they'd established infertility, the pregnancies had made the process more expensive. They needed to have three unsuccessful IUIs in a row before any payments would be applied to the deductible, and with each miscarriage, the count started again.

"We could afford it but barely," she said. "This shit is so expensive."

"Tell me about it," Chelsea said. "We cashed out part of my retirement just to have one kid."

"I'm thirty-two; I'm healthy; I feel like I should be able to have a baby, but when I talk like that, Liv doesn't like it."

"What does she want you to say?" McCray said.

Izzy shrugged. "Oh, you know, be grateful. Be happy. Maybe it's for the best, anyway, because kids are expensive and she's always traveling."

McCray scrunched up her face. "That's cold."

"No, she doesn't mean it that way. She's just one of those glass half full people."

Many of us had our own miscarriage stories, and we told Izzy to be gentle with herself and patient with Liv, that a thing like this could be hard on a couple—that each person would experience the loss in her own way.

"Exactly," Izzy said. "On some level, Liv is just never going to get how I feel."

A log fell in the fire and we all readjusted our chairs to avoid the new path of the smoke. Above the flames, clouds of long-tailed fish flies flitted.

"But you're doing better now?" Stacey said finally. "The therapy's helping?"

"I hope so," Izzy said in a voice that was not especially convincing. "It's not exactly in my plan to get divorced from my daughter's other mom."

The next day, armed with this new knowledge, we saw Izzy and Liv's interactions differently. Every difference of opinion between them became a threat, every gentle word or thoughtful gesture seemed like an effort to repair their fragile relationship. Many of us had been through rocky stretches in our own marriages—Annie and Regan, it turns out, had actually separated for a few months after Annie slept with someone else—and we understood how hard it could be when your kids were small just to have a moment alone together. For the next few nights, we took turns making the easy dinners we'd planned out ahead of time—veggie burgers, pasta, black bean quesadillas—and we volunteered to watch Hattie so that Izzy and Liv could walk on the beach or float together on a raft. We wanted this space away from their lives to offer a new start; we believed the right trip could turn things around.

On Thursday, it rained, and we had a long, loud day inside. There were more than a dozen kids—some old enough to do puzzles and crafts in the yoga room, but many kids were so young that they could not sit still or avoid tantrums. That night, after the kids were finally asleep and the adults were playing cards in the living room, Jenna said she was burned out and Beth suggested we take turns babysitting.

"Good idea," Alex said. "We can even go somewhere. There are hiking trails and fishing. We can also canoe down a river."

"Yes, that," McCray said. "Let's pack up a cooler of beer and float down the river."

We drew straws. Part of the group went to the river on Wednesday while the rest of us oversaw the snacks and sunscreen and sandcastles and naps; the next day we switched. The Thursday group filled two SUVs—nine adults and the three older kids who'd wanted to come along.

At Alex's family's lake house, filled with new age books and framed signs with inspirational quotes, it was easy to forget that we were in a small, conservative town in Michigan, but as soon as we pulled into the lot at the boat rental, it became clear again. This was not Traverse City with its storefronts of artisanal shops and steady influx of tourists from Chicago but a scattering of depressed townships where local families from Michigan vacationed. We were surrounded by oversized pickup trucks with gun racks and Trump stickers, sunburned men in muscle shirts and trucker hats. Alone any of us but Liv and McCray could probably pass for an outdoorsy kind of straight woman, but together our short hair and hiking clothes and lack of husbands became conspicuous, and the other people in the parking lot all seemed to be eyeing us with curiosity and suspicion.

"Are we going to be okay here?" Liv asked, her eyes scanning the people, the trucks, the metal sign with the rates for deer processing. "I don't exactly think we fit in."

Alex seemed uncharacteristically flustered. "Definitely," she said. "People around here might be rough around the edges, but they're good people."

She told us she'd been coming to this same river since she was a little girl and that her time "up north" had never been anything but wonderful, though, of course, her positive experiences proved nothing. She had never been here as half of a lesbian couple and with her round cheeks and light brown bob, she had the generically pretty look of a Midwestern mom.

Stacey raised an eyebrow and nodded at the small log building with a sign about boat rentals. "I nominate Alex and Izzy. You go in and we'll give you cash."

\ \ \ \ \ \ \

As we boarded the bus, a low-grade tension stayed with us and kept us quiet. We stared out the bus windows, watched the evergreen trees and gravel roads until the bus stopped and we saw the muddy patch of sand where we would launch our boats. Almost as soon as we were moving down the river, though, the feeling of nervousness evaporated so completely that we began to think we'd been paranoid. Of course people stared, just as many of us had stared at the Arab family we'd seen on one of our beach walks, two teenage girls boogie-boarding in Lake Huron in burkinis. We had not meant for our stares to signify disapproval—in fact, we'd been delighted—but we'd been surprised to see someone unexpected in such a quiet and homogeneous place.

We launched our boats at ten in the morning and by eleven, we were mildly buzzed from the fizzy wine and Michigan beer we'd packed in the coolers and we were beginning to relax. It was sunny and warm without being hot, the canoeing itself easy because we were paddling along with the current, and the river wasn't crowded. We joked around, ate Oreos and Cheez-Its. McCray and Chelsea had brought three brightly colored Super Soaker water guns, which the kids passed back and forth between the canoes and used to tag passing trees. A couple hours down the river, we pulled the canoes over to the riverbank to eat lunch. As we were getting ready to get back in our boats, Chelsea and McCray's son, Landon, a skinny nine-year-old with a blond buzz cut, convinced us all we should play assassin once we were back on the water. Liv, volunteered to manage the game, and gave each of us the name of a target. If we succeeded in shooting our target, the game paused so they could whisper the name of their target who would then become ours.

A few people switched places in the canoes and then we paddled to a wide deep curve in the river, where the current all but disappeared. One of Lindsay and Stacey's kids got the first hit but was then taken out by Chelsea who, with her mirrored sunglasses and thick muscled arms, managed to make the hot pink gun seem intimidating. She shot Alex, swam to Alex's canoe to get her new target, and then shot the girl who'd been sitting beside her. Before she could even aim at Izzy, though, Izzy jumped out of her canoe and disappeared underwater. When she reemerged a few seconds later, she was standing in the shallow water on the other side of the river where several unattended canoes littered the shore.

"How did she do that?" Chelsea said. "Is she a fish?"

"Synchronized swim team in college," Liv said. "Girl of many talents."

Landon got Lindsay, and then Izzy shot Stacey and ran to the riverbank. We heard someone whistle and looked up to see a group of guys in their midtwenties perched on a narrow rock ledge above the shore, drinking cans of beer and staring at Izzy who had stripped down to a black string bikini.

"Looking good," one of them called out. "You have a great ass."

He was a heavyset guy with a faint goatee, his bare chest mottled with sunburn. He seemed too drunk to be on a river, let alone near the edge of a cliff.

"It's a compliment, lady," he said. "You should say thank you."

Izzy ignored him and ducked back under the water toward Stacey's canoe and paused the game to get her new target. When the game restarted, Landon shot Chelsea but was soon taken out by Izzy. Then it was down to McCray, which made sense to us, and Izzy who didn't. We had never seen this competitive, athletic side of Izzy, and as she darted from the water to the shore, training her gun on McCray the whole time, we watched her with awe.

"All right, babe!" Liv shouted whenever she avoided getting hit. "Look at you."

When McCray leaned over the boat to refill her water gun, Izzy hit her arm right above the Super Mario tattoo, and we all cheered, and then Liv jumped in the water and swam toward her. When she reached the shore, she kissed her with more passion than she probably would have sober.

Lindsay and Stacey exchanged a mildly disapproving look, but McCray grinned at Chelsea. "I'm with Liv," she said. "There's nothing hotter than a good-looking woman who can shoot a gun."

We heard a hooting sound from one of the guys on the hillside and then a small rock landed just beside Liv and Izzy, followed by another. Liv and Izzy looked at each other in disbelief and then peered up at the hillside, where the guy who'd catcalled Izzy waved.

"Cut it out," Liv yelled. "What the hell?"

"Come on," Stacey said. "He's drunk. Let's go."

We had paddled over to them and were now just feet away. Another rock came toward them, and this time, Izzy screamed and picked up her foot.

"He hit me," she said. "Jesus Christ."

The same guy in the trucker hat laughed. "That's what you get," he said. "You should watch what you're doing."

A larger rock splashed in the water in front of them, and Izzy took Liv's hand and pulled her toward the canoe.

"Okay, man," we heard one of the guy's friends say. "Leave her alone."

For about twenty minutes, we paddled as hard as we could, and when it became clear that no one was following us, our fear gave way to anger. Lindsay was upset that all this had happened in front of her kids, Alex felt this had ruined an otherwise good trip and given us a bad impression of Michigan, and Liv thought someone should call the police.

"I don't care where we are," she said. "We can't let people get away with this crap."

McCray, though, had a plan. She wanted to pee in a water gun and hide out down the river. When the guys eventually caught up to us, we'd spray them with piss.

"You're joking, right?" Stacey said. "Obviously we aren't going to do that."

She shook her head and looked back and forth between Landon and McCray as if to say, "I can't believe you're acting like this in front of your child."

"She's joking," Chelsea said. "There will be no pee."

"Are you joking, Mama?" Landon said. "If you're not, I'll do the peeing."

McCray squeezed his shoulder. "I don't like bullies. That man should not have thrown rocks at Izzy."

We rounded a curve in the river and small houses began to appear on either side of the river, which Alex said meant we were about forty minutes from the parking lot.

"Just so I'm clear, that's a no on the pee plan, right?" Liv said. "I don't—"

Chelsea looked back at her wife. "McCray?"

McCray shrugged. "Whatever."

About thirty minutes later, once we were safely back in the giant black SUV we'd rented, out of earshot of Chelsea and McCray, Liv started laughing. "I can't believe that just happened."

"What part?" Alex said. "You mean the rocks?"

"The rocks. McCray. You know she was definitely not joking about the pee, either," she said. "Fifty bucks she's sprayed piss on someone with a Super Soaker before."

"Absolutely," we said. "Of course she has."

The gravel popped behind us as Alex pulled out of the lot.

Izzy and Liv were smiling at each other, but after a beat, Izzy's voice got almost wistful.

"I do like McCray, though," she said. "She seems kind and loyal. She's 100 percent the person who's grown on me the most."

/ / / / / / /

The canoe trip had not been the relaxing afternoon we'd planned, and yet, it seemed to have changed something between Izzy and Liv. For the rest of the trip, they held hands and joked around with each other, took showers together during Hattie's naps. On the last night, after the rest of the group had arrived in town but were now back at their hotels for the night, Izzy asked Beth if she would mind listening for Hattie so that she and Liv could swim, and then the rest of us saw them walk to the beach and go skinny-dipping—two dark shapes in the distance, running through the water together and laughing. The next morning, when they hugged us goodbye, their marriage seemed intact, and we were surprised when we heard a few months later that they were splitting up. The news came via Liv's Twitter feed—an image of a statement that looked like it had been written by a publicist. She was famous now—the movie about the families in Arkansas had earned an Oscar nomination for best supporting actress—and everything she posted was upbeat and professional.

"It was a mutual decision," the statement said. "Although we have decided to separate, we still have great love and respect for each other and remain partners in parenthood for our daughter, Hattie."

In spite of the generic language, we believed this part, too, until the following summer in a hotel pool in Bloomington, when Izzy told us that Liv was now living with the supporting actress from the Arkansas movie, that the two of them had been having an affair for more than a year.

"But that was last summer," we said. "Last summer you two seemed so happy."

"Well, I guess *she* wasn't happy," Izzy said.

Izzy had left Brooklyn to live with her mom in the suburbs of New Jersey, where she now worked at a mortgage company and had primary custody of Hattie, an arrangement that she and Liv had seemed to agree upon. Izzy was still prettier and more stylish than the rest of us, but she no longer seemed so different, and she thought it was funny when we told her how enamored we'd been with her and Liv when they'd first joined our group.

"We were pretty enamored with ourselves, too," she said. "We thought we had something figured out."

So we had been wrong about Liv. Why then was it so unsettling to read the interview Lindsay had found in *American Cinematographer*? Although the focus of the article was a different project, she also talked about the origins of the Arkansas movie and her interest in alternative families—how disconnected and lonely people were these days, what a beautiful venture it could be to expand your intimate circle beyond what felt comfortable.

"My daughter's donor family is this way," she said. "We meet sometimes, all of the donor families, and in any other context, we'd never know each other. Some of these people—we truly have nothing in common."

We hadn't seen her since the divorce and were surprised that she thought about us at all, though more surprised by what came next. She told the interviewer more than some of us had told our own families. How we had nicknamed the donor Jake Gyllenhaal because he had listed him as a look-alike on a form, that we'd seen two pictures of him as a child but none as an adult. She said he was older than some of the donors, twenty-eight, but he seemed kind and healthy. He had no family history of heart disease or high blood pressure, played soccer, loved dogs. His mother was a high school principal with green eyes, his father a dentist, his grandfather a tailor who'd immigrated from Hungary only to die in a car accident at age fifty-two. She'd taken a handful of facts and imagined this stranger's whole life.

"But it was basically chance," she said. "We picked this man we knew almost nothing about, and he helped make our wonderful daughter."

If the interview had ended there, we would have forgiven her for sharing our secrets, but she went on to tell the story of our trip to Michigan, which she had found to be strange and unnerving. She described the town as backwater, the people on the river as rednecks. She claimed—none of us had heard this happen—that the guy who'd been throwing rocks at her had also been yelling homophobic slurs. "And this woman I was with whose son is related to my daughter—her solution was to pee in a water gun and shoot it at him."

"So did she?" the interviewer wanted to know, but Liv said this wasn't the point.

She went on to say that she had little in common with most of us. We were suburban and conventional. We served our children nachos for dinner and dressed like the very worst lesbian stereotypes: shapeless T-shirts, bad haircuts. A few women in the group were Republicans.

"I would not in a million years choose some of these women to be my family," she said. "But, you know, you don't choose your parents either, and that's probably a good thing, right? We can't grow if we're not challenged."

The interview was over a year old, but we didn't find it until the height of the pandemic, all of us trapped at home, scrolling our phones, and maybe this was why her comments made us feel so lonely and deflated. We had just canceled that summer's meetup in Charleston and hadn't yet decided what, if anything, we'd do online instead. We had time to wonder by ourselves what had happened. Maybe Liv didn't think of us as people who read film magazines or maybe she had already decided she wouldn't see any of us again or maybe she was simply pointing out what had always been right there for us to see—we were bound to each other by almost nothing but will, free, at any time, to let go.

WHAT KIND
OF PERSON

After the baby died, a nurse removed the tubes and put his body in Emma's arms. Two pounds of translucent skin and bony limbs, a thin fuzz of dark brown hair. He wore a preemie diaper, a tiny blue knit hat, and matching booties that had come from a cardboard box in the corner of the NICU with a sign on it that read MADE WITH LOVE BY HICKORY GROVE BAPTIST CHURCH.

The adoptive parents had flown in from Flagstaff: a nearly forty-year-old woman and her slightly older husband, an elementary school teacher and an engineer. The woman wore large silver rings on most of her fingers; the man had a puffed beard the shape of a squirrel's tail. Emma had liked the pictures of their small mint green house with its yawning plants and terra-cotta tile, the gentleness she saw in their faces. When she handed the woman her son's body, she took him to a rocking chair by the windows, held him toward the winter sunlight, gazed at him so longingly that Emma had to look away. At least, this part—choosing them—she'd done right.

\ \ \ \ \ \ \

On the way home from the hospital, her dad stopped at a Panera and Emma and her parents ate thick hot sandwiches and soup served in bread bowls. It was midafternoon, the lunch crowd dispersing. In the booth behind them, a man laughed in long, loud gulps. Her mom said the doctors and nurses had done everything they could; she'd been impressed, considering. Her dad stood up, returned with three giant chocolate chip cookies. "Here," he said, pushing the butter-stained paper sleeve toward her. "Please."

Her parents were Southern Baptists and strict about it, especially her mother, but her pregnancy had begun a truce between them. They were not happy she had gotten pregnant, but they'd been even less happy about much of her life up until then. Before, she'd snuck out, smoked pot and done molly, skipped school so much she had nearly failed the tenth grade. After, she did what they told her to do. "You have a chance to start over," her mother had said. "You can decide again what kind of person it is you want to be."

There was a small funeral in the middle of the week, about a dozen people gathered around a tiny mound of dirt in the cemetery where her grandfather was buried, including the adoptive parents, who stood at the far edge of the crowd, crying. They'd named the baby Iggy, which did not sound like a real name to her, let alone a name for the small person she'd held, and every time the minister said it, she flinched. Liam, the birth father, said he would come and then didn't, which she tried not to take personally. He was not her boyfriend or even her classmate, and she knew his parents saw her as an obstacle to his otherwise bright future. When they'd told them about the pregnancy, his father had taken one long look at everything wrong with her—snarled hair, black boots, pink eyeliner—and demanded a paternity test.

\ \ \ \ \ \ \

After the funeral, her friends had no idea what to say to her, and so they offered her weed and nicotine and tried to distract her with gossip about Rylee Fitzgerald giving Andrew Nolan a hand job on the swim team bus, which just made Emma feel old and faraway. She began to spend mornings and lunches in a library carrel, flipping through travel magazines.

Meanwhile, adults she barely knew sent long emotional letters about their losses—miscarriages, a dead child, a forced adoption that had taken place decades ago. Last year's English teacher, Mrs. Snyder, who had caught her plagiarizing an essay from an Amazon review, gave her a book of poetry with lines underlined in shaky gray pencil. *Since I lost you, I am silence haunted.* Her mother's first cousin sent a card inviting Emma to come live with her family in Sioux Falls. *Maybe you'd like a change of scenery*, she wrote. *Probably this sounds crazy, but if it's appealing at all, please know I'm serious!* The letters gave her the feeling of company, but also left her with a sense of shame. If the baby hadn't died, he would have been raised by strangers, so how could she say she'd lost anything?

Once a week, she went to the same Christian therapist she'd gone to for a few months after her mom found her baggie of pills and weed in a tampon box in the bathroom. He was a heavyset man with thick eyebrows and a perfectly smooth head who talked a lot and always seemed proud of the wisdom he imparted. Because her relationship with Iggy had been ill-defined, he said she was suffering from what the experts termed "complicated grief."

"If I'd planned to keep him, it would be easier?"

He shook his head. "Different."

When she'd suggested raising the baby herself, her mother had admonished her to put another person's well-being above her own for once, and her father had agreed. "Not an option," he'd said. "Not even close."

"You won't always feel this bad," the therapist told her. "But it's going to take a while to feel better."

\ \ \ \ \ \

All that winter, she was patient. She practiced stoichiometry and differential equations; she wrote a ten-page research paper about *The Grapes of Wrath* without cheating. She helped the youth group raise money for a mission trip to Honduras. She took the SAT. She went through the motions. Throughout the motions she felt foggy and disconnected, but she held on to the women from the letters who had told her they had once been certain they could not keep going, that somehow, eventually, the grief stopped pulsing.

Then one afternoon in May, she went to the bathroom and overheard her mother outside on the front porch, talking with her aunt, Carla, who lived in Greensboro and had come to visit. She was angry but whispering. Her first thought was that someone was getting a divorce, but then she heard her name and sat very still on the lid of the toilet seat, her mother's voice rising up through the open window.

"I want to forgive her. I need to forgive her, but I can't," her mother said. "I can barely look at her."

Her aunt murmured words she couldn't hear, and then her mother was trying to say something else that kept getting choked out by tears.

"The thing is—" she said. "This sounds awful, but I can't shake the feeling that this was her fault."

Emma's hair on her arms bristled, and she felt her blood thrumming in her ears. These were her dark thoughts said out loud, and it was still a jolt to hear them spoken, especially from her mother who believed that tragedies happened for a reason. Her mother who had been right beside her when the doctor had said these things happened sometimes, that it was nobody's fault, that it happened more often than one might think.

"I just don't trust her," her mom said, her voice brighter now, almost gossipy. "*Who knows* what she was doing while she was pregnant? There's not a lot I'd put past this kid."

She went back to her bedroom and found her headphones, but the music didn't help her get rid of the feeling that her mother was right. Before she had known she was pregnant, it had been the summer of Liam. The summer of Juuling in the walk-in freezer at Chick-fil-A, feeling each other up behind the manager's back. The summer of smoking pot and racing around in his Jeep, their sleepy town of strip malls and tiny brick churches suddenly the backdrop of a new life. With Liam she was reckless, but it felt like bravery. Once, they had sex in a cemetery; another time, they drove all night to the beach with nothing but tabs of acid and a box of Pop-Tarts. They'd taken pills and used cans of whipped cream to do whippets. After the pregnancy test, she'd stopped everything cold turkey, but she hadn't known that she was pregnant until halfway through the second trimester. Or possibly, she had known—*should have* known—that her fatigue and weight gain meant something.

At dinner that night, she watched her mother attend to her with a practiced, even calm. Lasagna, salad, how was your day, and yet, it was also true what she had said on the porch—she couldn't look at her, not the way her father could, and Emma understood that her mother did not expect things between them to improve.

The card from Sioux Falls had a phone number and when she called it, a woman with a bright Southern accent answered the phone. Kristen. She had met her at her Aunt Carla's wedding when she was in middle school and remembered her as a thin, plain woman with glasses who danced in bare feet, but she couldn't picture her face.

"This is Emma," she said and then added her last name and her mother's name. "You sent me a card."

In the background a toddler squealed, and a man's voice answered in a teasing cadence that sounded like he was chasing the kid, goofing around. She was filled with a sudden panic that she had misunderstood, but before she could backtrack, Kristen made the same offer again.

"As long as you want," she said immediately. "Whatever we can do to help."

\ \ \ \ \ \ \

On the plane three weeks later, hovering above miles of green farmland and long straight roads, cocooned by the humming roar of the engine, she promised herself that in this new life she had been granted, she would find a way to make amends. She closed her eyes. Prayer, which she had resisted for most of her life, still felt like it belonged to someone else, but she was desperate. *Please help me,* she prayed, her first prayer since the days in the hospital's chapel, kneeling in front of a makeshift altar beside old women whose husbands were dying. *Give me a sign, God. Show me what you want me to do, and I'll do it. Let me give you my life and make it be of use.*

Kristen and her husband, Jason, lived in an old three-bedroom house on the edge of a city park of ballfields and splash pads lined with towering oaks. Kristen stayed home with their two little kids, and Jason worked as a research analyst north of the city in the government geological lab that had brought their family to South Dakota six years before. The house was small and the carpeted floors covered in LEGO pieces and Magna-Tiles more often than not, but Emma liked being swallowed up by the family's everyday routines—breakfast, walk, naptime, playtime, dinner. Pancakes on Saturday morning, family hike in the afternoon. It was only at night, when she woke up sweating and terrified, that the house felt like it belonged to strangers.

One night in August, after the kids were in bed, Kristen and Jason sat her down at the dining-room table and said they wanted to talk. The summer was almost over, and they wanted to know if she would enroll in the local high school for her senior year.

"We're in a good district," Kristen said. "Just think about it."

She thought *yes* but said, "I don't know. If this is going to be long-term, I'm going to need a chore list. Either that or I get a job and pay rent."

This made them both laugh, though Emma was serious. She was indebted to them, and it was beginning to feel like a burden. She'd displaced the two-year-old from her bedroom; she was one more person sharing one bathroom, eating meals, making dishes; and she didn't understand the motivation behind this unyielding kindness. They didn't know her; they were barely related. And, as far as she could tell, they weren't even religious, which was what she had found usually explained unconditional generosity.

"I don't understand why you're helping me."

Jason looked at Kristen and then back at Emma. "You're easy to like, and we're happy to have you here."

He reached for a water glass from dinner, coated in condensation, took a sip, and gave her a long reassuring smile that made her wonder if he and Kristen knew anything at all about her past.

"You're very kind, but it's a little overwhelming, sometimes," she said. "As you may know, I haven't always been a good person."

Jason started to contradict her, and Kristen put her hand on his arm. They waited for her to continue, but it was hard to explain. There were the drugs, yes, and the times she'd stolen money right from her mother's wallet, but the part that stayed with her was the intolerance she'd had for her parents' pain. Because their rules were sometimes unreasonable, it had been hard for her to see their emotion as anything but manipulation. She was haunted now by the image of her mother sitting on the bottom step of their stairs in her flannel pajamas, shaking. One of many late-night arguments that ran together, except this time, her mother wouldn't stop sobbing, kept saying over and over that she was out of ideas, that she didn't know what else to do.

"It's just very important for me to help," Emma said, finally. "Please."

Jason and Kristen exchanged a look, and then Kristen got the magnetic notepad from the fridge that said *Food & Stuff* in curling green script.

"Okay," she said. "Let's make a chore list."

/ / / / / / /

Emma spent her last weeks of summer wondering how she'd explain her living circumstances to her new classmates, but the high school turned out to be so large that no one noticed she was new. At the Baptist school she had attended since pre-K, a school that had very nearly kicked her out twice before she'd gotten pregnant—not getting kicked out after that had required three meetings with the principal and a promise not to host a baby shower or otherwise make her condition seem "appealing"—there had been around fifty other students in her whole grade. Here the hallways were filled with bodies filing past in a constant roar of voices, and it was easy to slink away from the crowd and stay anonymous. It felt as if the past year of her life should be visible on her body, but no one gave her a second look.

She wasn't sure of her place in this new environment and prayed for a sign. When she saw a flier in a restroom stall announcing a meeting of the Gay-Straight Alliance, she wondered if this might be it. A picture of rainbow-colored balloons that said, *Allies welcome. Please help make South Dakota safe for all of us!* She thought of a sermon she'd heard that included a story about a woman who asked God for a father for her child. "I don't care if you have to send me someone from Alaska," the woman had prayed, and a week later, she met a man who was on leave from an army base in Anchorage. God listened, the preacher had said, *and* he had a sense of humor. Perhaps, she thought, she had asked for a sign of how she could help, and God had sent a literal one.

That night after dinner, she handed her phone to Kristen and showed her a picture of the flier. "I was thinking of going," she said. "I wanted to make sure it's okay with you."

Her parents considered themselves to be tolerant, but they didn't like for gay people to have children or to hold hands or kiss each other in public, and they also thought that trans people were suffering from mental disorders. In her high school, there had been no openly gay or trans students, let alone an alliance between them and the straight students, but she had often felt a kinship with gay people. Growing up she had always tried to do what she was supposed to do, but her mere presence seemed to irritate her mother and her teachers. She got in trouble for her tone of voice, her lack of attention, the provocative way her uniform hung on her body. She understood what it meant to be unalterably different from how she was supposed to be.

Kristen put down the cooking magazine she'd been reading, pulled her feet up on the couch, and crossed her legs. "I'm bisexual, you know," she said. "I've never had a girlfriend, but it's a part of who I am, and I'm happy about it."

Emma felt her face burning. She had the uneasy feeling that Kristen was going to tell her something about her sex life with Jason, which she already heard sometimes faintly through her bedroom wall, and willed her to stop.

"If you want to join a GSA, I think that's great."

"I'm not—" Emma said. "I'd be going as an ally."

Kristen shrugged. "As far as I'm concerned, whoever you are in that department is terrific."

/ / / / / / /

The GSA turned out to be about a half dozen awkward students who sat around in a circle each week in Mr. Hansen's physics classroom. A few of them had streaks of purple and pink in their hair, and many dressed in shapeless mismatched ensembles that looked as if they'd been borrowed from thirty-something gamers. First, they shared their pronouns and sexuality and then they spent the rest of the time talking about what they'd done over the summer. Everyone but Emma said they were bi, including a skinny redheaded freshman named AJ who also said, "trans." The ringleader seemed to be a cherub-faced girl named Kate, a junior with a tiny silver septum ring who wore her dark hair in an undercut with a zigzag cut into the back and who seemed more confident, if not more popular, than the other students.

"We accomplish things, you know," she assured Emma the next day at lunch. "Just not until February. Until February, it's basically like queer kid social club."

"Valentine's Day?"

This made Colton, the other person at their lunch table, laugh. He was also a junior and in ROTC, which he said he pretty much hated but hoped would pay for college.

"No," Kate said. "The legislative session."

She explained that in recent years, South Dakota had become the place for anti-LGBTQIA+ groups to test their bills before they tried to pass them in other states. It was very conservative here for one thing, she said, but also it was also cheap to advertise, and, because the legislative session was so short, the process was quick. In February, Kate said, there would be at least one anti-LGBTQIA+ bill, because there was always at least one bill, and it would likely have something to do with trans kids. Probably the bill wouldn't pass, but the GSA would take a bus to Pierre anyway and testify because the governor was in the Tea Party and liable to do anything, and these bills did threaten vulnerable people, and it wasn't a good idea to get complacent.

"Wow, okay," Emma said, unsure if she was impressed or overwhelmed.

"She's a nerd," Colton said. "Ask what her GPA is."

Kate rolled her eyes and turned back toward Emma. "It's easy to act like it's just this big show that doesn't matter, but it does," she said. "Sometimes these laws pass. Everything matters."

\ \ \ \ \ \ \

Every Saturday morning, her dad called. Twenty minutes of talking about nothing—a rainstorm, a pancake breakfast fundraiser at the church—and then he'd ask if she was okay and if she needed money and handed the phone to her mom who would repeat a shorter version of the same details and then ask to talk to Kristen. A few weeks into the school year, though, he said that her mom was out at the grocery store and that she was having a hard time. Her job was turning out to be too much for her lately, and so she'd put in her notice. She was preoccupied, and Emma shouldn't take it personally if she didn't hear from her for a while.

"Is her knee worse?"

Her mom had arthritis, which made her work as a preschool teacher challenging, but she had an assistant and so far, she'd been managing okay.

"No," her dad said and paused for what felt like a long time. "It's just the kids. She just can't be around kids right now."

Her mother had worked at the same preschool since Emma had been a student there, and it was hard to imagine her mother doing anything else. She was the type who spent weekends at yard sales buying puzzles and toys for her classroom, the type of teacher who parents credited with turning their unruly three- and four-year-olds into well-behaved children.

"Will she retire?"

"Oh, she'll do something," her dad said. "Eventually she'll find something else."

/ / / / / / /

At the next GSA meeting, Colton waited until Mr. Hansen stepped out in the hallway and then clapped his hands and said that he had an announcement.

"So, my future stepmother lives in Dell Rapids," he said. "And, as we all know, our good friend Schaefer lives in Dell Rapids."

Everyone nodded. Schaefer was a conservative state senator who frequently sponsored anti-gay bills and often implied in his interviews about them that gay and trans people were predators. To make things worse, Schaefer was only thirty-six, younger than most of their parents, and proof that the bad ideas were not simply going to die out.

"So, as it turns out, our friend Schaefer," he said, pausing dramatically, "is in the same neighborhood, three houses down."

"Okay," AJ said. "I don't get it."

"We know where he lives," Colton said. "So now we can do something."

Kate, who had obviously already heard this information from Colton, said that she saw his point, that Schaefer was an asshole who deserved to have his life disrupted, but they should be careful.

"We can't vandalize his house, obviously," she said, "and if we want to talk to him, we'll see him at the town hall meetings."

"I'm not saying vandalize," Colton said. "I'm just saying, we do something. Ring a doorbell, leave a note."

"You know his other big issue is guns, right?" AJ said. "I'm personally not trying to get shot."

Then Hansen came back and the conversation ended. Over the course of the next several days, though, a plan developed. That weekend, before it got any colder, they would go raiding, which meant sneaking around houses at night and throwing feed corn. It was like toilet papering, Colton explained, but not as mean. The birds ate the corn, and, as long as you didn't hurl whole ears of corn at windows, nothing got damaged.

"Plus, he'll know what's happening," he said. "It's a pretty recognizable sound. It's not like he's going to think he's being robbed."

"And then we leave a note," Kate said. "We'll say, *It sucks to not feel safe, doesn't it? It sucks not to have your private life respected.*"

As the only trans person in their group, AJ's vote counted more than everyone else's, and though he looked impatient, Colton heard him out. AJ said he didn't mind being mean and he didn't mind telling Schaefer exactly what he thought of his stupid ideas, but he didn't want things to get worse.

"I just feel like it could backfire," he said. "He already thinks we're freaks. I don't want to help him prove his point."

Everyone nodded along, but within a few minutes, the original plan was back on the table and moving forward. They'd go the following weekend; Colton and Kate would get corn from their grandparents' farms. It was important, Kate said, for Schaefer to think about the impact of his actions, to imagine for a moment what it would feel like to be constantly and relentlessly harassed.

"Do you know why this asshole got into politics?" Kate asked Emma. "No."

"He wanted to change the custody laws so he and other fathers paid less child support," she said. "*This* is our Mr. Family Values."

That Saturday, Emma dressed in dark clothing and told Kristen and Jason that she was going to a movie in Dell Rapids with some friends—an excuse Kate had come up with that would explain their location for the parents who tracked their phones. They didn't question her story or ask why it was they weren't just going to a movie in Sioux Falls. Instead, they asked if she needed money or a car to borrow, what time it was she thought she'd be home. They'd be up early the next morning for a Friends and Family Day at the research lab.

"I'm not sure," she said, which was true, she'd forgotten to plan this part. "If it's going to keep you up, I don't have to go."

"No, no," Kristen said. "Just let us know if you'll be home after midnight. We'll keep our phones on."

When Kate texted to say that they were outside the house, Emma was in the living room with Jason and Kristen who were snuggled up together on the couch watching Netflix, and she didn't get up right away. There was time still, maybe, to change her mind. In her old life, she had lied to her parents constantly without thinking much about it, but now she felt guilty.

Jason paused the television and peeked through the venetian blinds. "I see headlights," he said. "Off you go. Have fun."

/ / / / / / /

Dell Rapids was a suburb about forty miles north of the city, and they were quickly past the sprawl of Sioux Falls shopping centers and malls and zooming along a two-lane highway lined on either side by farmhouses and cornfields. Kate was driving, Colton was up front navigating, and Emma was in the back with AJ, her face pressed to the window while Colton's hip-hop mix blared through the speakers. Colton directed Kate off the highway to a narrow dimly lit street of RVs and small houses and a school parking lot where they hid the car behind a school bus. They each filled their pockets with handfuls of corn, and then Colton took a small backpack that held the rest.

"It's a little walk," he said. "He's just on the next street over."

They followed him to a small subdivision of large, newly constructed ranch houses, sitting on huge lots of land with pickup trucks in most of the driveways. Just beyond the neighborhood lay farmland, but this stretch of houses looked more crowded and suburban than Emma had been expecting. Just past the first few houses, Colton pointed to a large gray house at the end of the cul-de-sac, and AJ stopped walking.

"It's too exposed," he said. "No way."

The house was at least twenty feet from its only set of neighbors, but the only trees in the yard were young and small, leaving them few hiding places. A streetlight a few houses down cast long beams of light across the grass.

Colton shrugged. "What's he going to do?"

"We'll split up," Kate said. "It will be fine."

AJ seemed unconvinced, but when Colton started walking, he followed. The plan was for Kate to tape the letter to the front door first and for everyone else to surround the house. When she was done, she'd throw the first handful of corn and this sound would signal everyone else. As soon as Schaefer reacted, they'd run back to the car.

The house was built into a hillside with a three-car garage and a porch out front. AJ and Colton ran past a basketball hoop and past the garage; Emma followed Kate to the side of the house closest to the porch and then kept running by herself, past a stone retaining wall and looped garden hose to a concrete patio at the back of the house with a brick firepit in the center of a circle of deck chairs. She stood with her back to the siding and tried to catch her breath. In the middle of the backyard sat a gray storage shed and at the far edge of the property rows of tall evergreens stood that would hide her while she escaped to the next neighborhood. After a few minutes, she heard the sound of corn raining down on glass. This was supposed to be her signal to throw her corn against the house, but instead she quietly dropped it on the patio and started walking toward the side yard. Before she made it, Kate sprinted past her to the other side of the house. Then Emma heard the screen door open and a man's voice shouting, "Get the fuck off my property."

It was quiet for a moment and then she heard more corn falling on the windows and then Schaefer was shouting. "All right," he said. "I warned you."

The door opened again, and Colton yelled, "Run!"

Emma made it to the side yard in time to see Colton and Kate race across the open grass toward a parallel street that would probably, eventually, take them back to their car. She stood up and walked in the shadows of the house until she could make sure that no one was watching her, but then she heard the crack of the rifle, followed by a loud thump.

"You come out or I keep shooting," Schaefer yelled. "The ball's in your court."

Her mind told her to run, but her body wouldn't go. She slid down against the house and sat still. The ground was cold and damp, but her legs were shaking.

"Okay," a voice called out. "Okay. Okay."

It was AJ—the smallest and youngest person in the group. If it had been up to him, they probably wouldn't even be here.

"You think this is funny?" Schaefer said.

"No."

"Well guess what, punk? Your friends left you, and now you're here with me."

He wasn't shouting anymore, but his voice had the aggression of an authority figure who'd been embarrassed and wanted to make a point.

"What's going to happen now," he said, "is that you clean up my yard."

What he seemed to have in mind was a slow and humiliating process: AJ picking up kernels of corn one by one while Schaefer followed behind him with a rifle. It was a power trip, and also her opening to leave. AJ would be okay—he wasn't the type to escalate things—but also, he was only fourteen, and she knew he'd be panicking the whole time, wondering if Schaefer would guess he was trans and lash out. The least she could do was make sure that he wasn't alone.

"There's someone back here," she shouted. "I'm walking toward you. Please don't shoot."

Schaefer seemed shorter than he had in pictures but also stockier. He had a thick mustache and was wearing an insulated flannel shirt and carrying a long rifle pointed at the ground. When he saw her, he almost smiled. "Your girlfriend didn't leave you after all."

"He's my little brother," Emma said. "And being here was my idea."

"I don't care whose idea it was," he said. "I want the two of you to clean this up."

They picked up corn from the front porch and the grass on the side of the house. When they got to the patio where Emma had hidden and emptied her pockets, Schaefer brought out an old broom from the toolshed. His role was to swing his phone's flashlight across the ground and point out the kernels they'd missed. She imagined he was the type of uncompromising father who congratulated himself for enforcing all of his many rules.

"I'm not punishing you," he said. "This is just you fixing a problem you created."

When they finally made it back to the front of the house, Schaefer said that he had decided not to call the police but that he hoped they'd learned a lesson.

"Yes, sir," AJ said right away. The light from the porch shone on his face and showed little droplets of sweat along his hairline even though it was cold. Behind him, the front door was open, and the note was still there on the glass, folded once.

"What lesson?"

"Actions have consequences," AJ said. "I understand that, and I'm sorry."

Hearing what sounded like genuine remorse in AJ's voice sent a flare of anger through her chest, and she made herself breathe in a long deep breath.

Schaefer turned to Emma. "I don't want to see you again. Understood?"

They had come to the end of this finally; he was ready to let them go, but she knew that if she didn't say something, she'd hate herself.

"This wasn't random," she said. "We know who you are."

"Let me guess," he said, looking at her hoodie and her Vans. "You think you're a lesbian."

He was so sure of himself that she understood he was used to these complaints. He had made himself famous by fighting against equality; pissing off gay people proved he was making progress.

"Yes," she said, her heart pounding. "That's right."

"You should be thanking me then. You don't see it now, but I'm trying to help you."

He seemed to believe what he was saying but that was almost worse.

"You need to do better," she said. "You're living your life in the wrong way."

Schaefer laughed. "Okay, honey," he said. "Right back at you."

On the car ride home, AJ retold each moment of the story. Everyone else seemed determined to hear it as a triumph, but what she kept thinking was that he'd had a gun, that they'd expected him to have a gun, and that they'd gone anyway. They'd put the path of their lives in danger for no real reason, and luckily, miraculously, they'd been okay.

When she got home, it was almost midnight and the house was dark and quiet. On the bathroom mirror, Kristen had left a sticky note that said they'd be leaving at 7:30 for the Family Day at the research center if she wanted to come. She brushed her teeth and splashed water on her face and then lay in bed, composing a text message to her mother. *My choices can't be undone, and I know they've caused us both a lot of pain. A nurse told me that it was probably not my fault that Iggy died, but I did drugs in the early weeks and of course we'll never know. I live with this, but I'm trying to be a better person.* She didn't send it, but she would, eventually.

/ / / / / / /

The next morning Jason drove them all to a research lab in the middle of miles and miles of cornfield with a security guard out front who looked at everyone's ID. Jason showed them the desk of monitors on the third floor where he tracked the size and shape of the earth's landforms and then they went back to the first floor and walked through the exhibits with the rest of the families—images of wildfires in Arizona, rainforest in South America, maps of arable land in North America. A collection of monitors at the entrance showed the images the satellites were gathering in real time from all over the world, cameras sliding along the beaches of Mozambique, the mountains of Colorado, the Black Sea.

"Look," Kristen said and pointed toward a monitor. "That's where tigers live."

The images looked less like photographs and more like brown and blue and green shapes that could be anywhere. It wasn't the pictures they were after, Jason said, but the finely calibrated data, gathered over and over, every sixteen days the size and shape of the whole world captured before it became something new.

DEAR MATT

I'm writing to apologize. I shouldn't have called your religion a cult or said my sister was an idiot for marrying you. I'm sorry. As I'm sure you know, she hasn't responded to any of my texts or calls or letters, and I'm not expecting you to convince her to talk to me, I just wanted to apologize to you directly and to explain a few things such as the vodka, which I got highly discounted at the Duty Free in Virginia and didn't realize was in violation of the University of Utah's married student housing policy. I did not fly across the country to pick a fight with you but to be with Ella before the baby was born, and, yes, to flee my apartment while my ex-fiancée and her aggressively heterosexual boyfriend moved her belongings out of my life and into his.

From your perspective, I'm sure it seems like my anger came out of nowhere, but, honestly, until this trip, I didn't take your relationship as seriously as you might think. Ella has always had boyfriends, and, with the exception of our childhood neighbor, Sam Allenwood, who is still in love with her and who I was secretly hoping she'd return to, I never paid much attention to any of them. You might think her marrying you would have been a clue that she planned to be with you for the long haul, but because my parents and I weren't allowed inside the temple to see the official ceremony for ourselves, it never felt entirely real. I figured the marriage was your idea and that my sister had just gone along with it. When she got pregnant a few months after the wedding and gave up the swimming scholarship that had brought her to Salt Lake City in the first place, I assumed the pregnancy was accidental. It wasn't until my visit when I saw Ella laugh at your jokes and squeeze your hand under the table that I realized this was her real and actual life, the one she wanted and meant to keep.

One of the last things you said to me was that I'm not Ella's mother. Do you remember this? We were in the courtyard behind the student apartments you were renting from the university, and I was threatening to stay in a hotel for my last night but hoping someone would stop me. "She's an adult," you told me. "Her religion is none of your business." You were on the walkway by the playground, whispering at me as if this would trick me into lowering my voice, but your self-consciousness only made me angrier.

"*She* is my business," I shouted. "Her well-being is always my business."

I was, as my therapist would say, emotionally dysregulated—heart galloping, breath tight, skin prickling—and my mind was feeding me insults faster than I could shout. At twenty, Ella was still impulsive, still prone to stupidity, barely an adult; you had ruined her swimming career for a life of board games and potluck dinners and proselytizing; you had no business getting her pregnant while you were both still broke and in college. As you may remember, I insulted Disneyland, your Hawaiian shirt collection, the gigantic staged wedding portraits displayed above your couch, your friend Levi, the pork buns your mom made for the baby shower. I did not say I was heartbroken, that by convincing my sister to join a religion that hated gay people so much they had briefly threatened to excommunicate kids who wouldn't disavow their gay parents, I was essentially losing my sister.

When Ella was born, I was four. Her birth was somewhat complicated—she was positioned feet first and delivered by cesarean; our mother developed tachycardia and an infection and the two of them stayed in the hospital longer than expected. In my memory, they were gone for a long time, but in reality, it was probably a few days, certainly no more than a week. Our father slept on a chair in the hospital room—my parents were still generally happy at that point—and I stayed with my maternal grandparents who fed me Klondike bars and let me watch Disney movies but were nevertheless not my parents. At night, I lay awake, listening to the furnace heave on and off, and held my breath while I watched the clock. If I could make it for one minute without breathing, I told myself, my parents would come. While I was supposed to be tracing my letters, I closed my eyes and prayed my dad would pick me up at the end of the day. On some level, I must have sensed the fragility of our family because, within a year, he moved out.

I tell you this story because I arrived in Utah feeling similarly abandoned by Ella—the person in my family who I'd always liked and relied on most. In the fifteen months or so that she'd been with you, she'd already become less available to me—unlikely to answer spontaneous phone calls, no longer interested in using her college breaks to visit. Between the pressure of law school and the end of my relationship with Hailey, it had been a difficult year, and Ella wasn't there. I was starting to wonder if her absence was more than the self-involvement of new love—if, in fact, she had stopped valuing my place in her life.

When I saw you in May, I was not in a good headspace. Hailey's furniture and most of her belongings were still in the apartment we'd shared, but I'd been living alone for a month, eating Lance peanut butter crackers and slushies from Sheetz, crying until my eyelids swelled. My last semester of law school was fairly easy, but I was struggling to focus, and I was worried about the bar exam. With Hailey gone, I couldn't sleep, and my body ached. I couldn't stop picturing her with the bartender she'd left me for—a chipper, shaggy-haired guy named Oliver who spent his free time rock climbing, traveling abroad to rock climb, and promoting little known brands of sunglasses and workout gear on social media. I had known he had a crush on Hailey but saw this less as a threat and more as proof of my good fortune.

I'd landed a summer associate position at a law firm in Raleigh that I hoped would offer me a full-time job, but because of her speech therapy externship and part-time job at the co-op, Hailey would stay in Charlottesville. I couldn't complain. She had already followed me from our small liberal arts college in Tennessee to Virginia, applied to this specific graduate program so we could live in the same place, and planned to move with me again to wherever I got a job after graduation. We would be just a few hours away for a couple months, which was nothing compared to our ten months of long-distance during her last year in college and my first year of law school. I knew already how much I'd miss her, though, and the night before I left, I proposed with a PowerPoint projected onto the wall in our living room. It began with a selfie of us at the beach-themed frat party in college where we'd first made out behind a giant unicorn pool float and then took a photo journey through the progression of our relationship—the Outward Bound trip where I'd first said I loved her, the first year she'd come home with me for Thanksgiving, our first night in our own place in Virginia, unpacking boxes. I listed qualities of hers that I admired: generosity, beauty, athleticism, sense of humor. I even included a slide of the counterbalancing arrows clipart with her name on one arrow and mine on the other. Our differences were a good thing; we balanced each other out.

It was, I see now, an argument for us to stay together. In the past year we'd been adjusting to living together—she listened to music constantly, invited friends over without telling me; I prioritized sleep over sex, studying over fun—but we were also figuring out who we were in this new place, at this particular moment in our lives. In college, Hailey seemed to think that I was smart and worldly, admirably liberal and ambitious, but these days (I suspected she'd been influenced by the socialist coworkers she'd befriended at the food co-op) she seemed to think I was too boring and traditional. Why did I care so much about money? What exactly did I love so much about studying the laws of an unjust system? When would be the time when I would slow down and enjoy myself? I accused her of being immature and short-sighted, of not appreciating the life I was trying to build for the two of us. When we were in the midst of an argument, I wondered if our relationship was harder than it should be, but when things were good, I thought our disagreements were helping us grow.

I knelt down in front of the couch and asked the question again. She was crying, and I truly didn't know if she was happy or about to break up with me.

"You sound nervous," she said and swiped at her tears.

"Well, I've put myself out there," I said. "If you say no, I'm going to be sad."

She laughed and kissed me. "Of course, the answer is yes," she said. "Who else would I marry if I didn't marry you?"

About a month later, when she began hiking and rock climbing with Oliver, a flash of jealousy flickered through me but died out quickly. I was busy with work and often out late with the other summer associates, and I trusted Hailey, a natural athlete and avid hiker who I thought was much likelier to have a crush on Oliver's gear and expertise than on him. Before me, she'd had two boyfriends and no girlfriends, but she still didn't seem that bisexual to me. She didn't like to watch TV shows unless they had a lesbian storyline, she never seemed especially flattered by the many men who flirted with her, and she'd told me many times how glad she was that I was not a man. We felt sorry for our female friends who deferred to their supposedly progressive boyfriends, our mothers who prepared for their surgeries by freezing meals for their husbands. With the exception of one night in July when Hailey called me drunk and crying, apologizing (I thought irrationally) for our summer apart, nothing unusual happened that summer, and when I came home in August, we began to plan our wedding. It wasn't until Christmas break when I heard her phone dinging in the night that I saw a flirtatious text from Oliver hovering above the lock screen. I used the passcode Hailey had given me years ago and never changed and found a string of explicit text messages between them going all the way back to July. We broke up that night, got back together that week, and then, a few months later, she left me for Oliver.

I have told a few friends about my idea for a support group for women whose bisexual girlfriends leave them for men, and they consider this to be a very funny joke. "Good one," a friend said. "We also need a group for women who catch their lapsed Catholic boyfriends praying." In their eyes, Hailey had betrayed me only by cheating. If I told them how crazy it makes me to imagine her holding hands with Oliver, traveling around the world with him, gathering the goodwill of being a beautiful straight couple, they would simply call this jealousy. Hailey has not blocked me on social media, and so I know she's not only still with Oliver but also engaged. From the pictures of shakshuka and Kung Pao tofu dinners, hikes with Oliver's dog, and the July Fourth cookout in her parents' backyard in Mississippi, you would guess the two of them had been together for ages. You would see no evidence at all of the four years she spent with me.

Our wedding was supposed to be this coming November at a horse farm in the Shenandoah Valley, and her father, a heavyset man with a close-cropped white beard, a beautiful singing voice, and a love of bass fishing and Aerosmith, was not planning to come. Although he seemed to like me well enough—he'd taken us fishing and camping a couple of times, and I'd been to several holidays at their house—this did not change his opposition to same-sex marriage. Of course this bothered Hailey—how could it not?—but this isn't why she left me. According to her, I was too conventional, too temperamentally drawn to worry. What she wanted was a happy and adventurous life.

"What do you think *I* want?" I said. "What the hell do you think I'm working so hard for?"

But it was too late; she had made up her mind.

"I still love you," she told me. "But when I'm with you, I'm just not happy."

Sometimes, I torture myself by imagining how things could have turned out differently. If I hadn't spent the summer in Raleigh, if I'd gone to her friend Wynter's wedding, if I'd complained less, had more sex, or agreed to get a cat, then maybe we'd still be together. Most of the time, though, I think our breakup was probably inevitable. Hailey didn't like her life with me, didn't like herself when she was with me, and even if I could have convinced her to stay, I'm not sure that I would go back and try. The estrangement between me and Ella on the other hand, feels unnatural and harder to accept. When I delude myself into imagining we can still be as close as we once were, though, I remember my last night in Utah, Ella's blank face, not responding.

I didn't like your friend Levi from the beginning—he was condescending and talked too much; I also resented the fact that we were having to chaperone a twenty-two-year-old's date—but if he hadn't tried to sell me on "religious freedom," I would have kept my mouth shut.

"Utah is a real leader in terms of gay rights," he said to me, during a break between Codenames and Yahtzee, a statement sparked it seemed, by him trying to make conversation with a gay person. "I don't know why other states don't just follow our model."

Ella was in the bathroom and you were in the kitchen getting snacks. He went on to explain a 2015 compromise that provided anti-discrimination laws for gay and trans people in exchange for "religious freedom." The LDS leaders were reasonable, he said. They didn't want people losing their jobs or housing, but they also needed to be able to practice their religion without interference.

"You mean the freedom to discriminate?"

His date looked uncomfortable, but he kept going. He thought it was sensible for a religion to have restrictions. He didn't think The LDS Church was any worse than any other Christian denomination.

"We're just the ones it's okay to hate," he said. "Nobody would make fun of a Jewish person anymore, but it's totally fine to say whatever you want about us."

I stared at him. Was he joking? Did he read the news?

"Okay," I said. "But a lot of queer kids in your church kill themselves, and you might want to ask why."

At this point, you and Ella returned, looking bewildered. I'm not sure what you'd heard us say, but I knew you could feel the tension between us. I looked at Ella and then back at Levi whose neck was turning red.

"Eventually," I said, "you have to decide where you stand."

He nodded, as if he agreed, but then mumbled that it wasn't his place, or mine, to question his religion's stance on homosexuality. I flinched, but you didn't and neither did my sister. Then he said, as if he had not started this conversation, that he'd rather not talk about religion or politics.

"This isn't religion or politics," I said, locking eyes with Ella. "What we're talking about is me."

At that moment, I had many options other than grabbing the vodka from my room and swigging it in front of you. I could have taken a walk or suggested another board game. I could have called a friend. I can only say that I wasn't thinking rationally. I felt that my sister had rejected me or, at least, failed to stand up for me, and I was ready to burn everything down.

On my last day in Salt Lake City, I woke up in my airport hotel with a heavy, guilty feeling. I'd destroyed my relationship with my fiancée and now with my sister. I'd already texted an apology, and Ella hadn't responded. My flight wasn't until the evening and so, after loading up on pastries and coffee from the hotel's breakfast bar, I rented a car and drove through the Wasatch Mountains to a hiking trail south of the city. I couldn't remember ever hiking without Hailey, but according to the guidebook I'd flipped through in the hotel lobby, this was what people did when they visited Utah. When I got to the trailhead at seven, the parking lot was nearly full, but for most of the hike the only people I saw were a couple in matching blue sun hats with a blond teenager who had a bad case of razor burn. We kept passing each other because they were faster than me but stopped at every overlook. They were friendly, but I felt slightly awkward because I guessed from the woman's BYU T-shirt and conservatively cut wind pants that they were LDS and even a stranger can take one look at my hair and tattoos and guess that I'm gay. Maybe they didn't care and probably wouldn't say anything if they did, but you never know.

Online the hike had been described as moderate, but it was more challenging than any of the hikes I'd taken in Virginia, and I was quickly out of breath. The sun was bright, the air warm. The high altitude left me parched and winded and I hadn't brought more than the small plastic water bottle I'd picked up at the hotel breakfast bar. I felt foolish, but also proud of myself for venturing out alone and pushing myself out of my comfort zone. At the first waterfall, I was enjoying the cool breeze lifting from the water, thinking about cutting my hike short, when the same family caught up with me again and stopped. The man wanted to know if I was visiting from far away—he'd seen me taking pictures—and when I said yes, the woman asked if I knew about the second waterfall. When I explained that I hadn't prepared for a longer hike, they offered to share their water with me. We went back and forth with me refusing and them insisting, and then the man took out a giant thermos to refill my bottle, and the woman handed me a Ziploc baggie of homemade trail mix. We hiked along the dusty trails for what felt like a long time until we eventually reached a steep rock incline that led to a waterfall.

We chatted most of the way but kept it light—the weather, the beauty of Utah's mountains and canyons, the fact that my sister had been recruited to the University of Utah's swim team. They had both grown up in the small town in Utah County where they still lived. The man worked as an engineer but said he had the day off. I got the sense there was a story about why—a funeral, maybe, a doctor's appointment, or some other private family issue that would also explain the boy's absence from school—but he didn't share it, and I didn't say anything about my argument with you and Ella or my breakup with Hailey, even though I was thinking of her with every step. There is a specific loneliness that comes with this kind of partial togetherness, where you are with another person but not with your whole self. This is what drives people to come out in the first place. On this day, though, I was just happy for their kindness and content not to be alone. At the top of the mountain, I took their family's picture, and they took mine, my hand waving in the air, jagged rocks and pine trees behind me. The hike back was downhill and faster, the sun bright but not too hot. When we reached the parking lot, we waved goodbye and that was that.

Two weeks ago, I was at a Harris Teeter in Raleigh, debating between two bags of salad greens when I saw a text from my mom. I had taken the bar exam a few days before and was still exhausted from studying and a little disoriented by my new life, and even though I was also lonely, I wasn't especially eager to text with my mom who, as you know, often requires a lot of emotional energy. When I saw the picture of Ella and your daughter in the hospital, I would like to say that my first thought was happiness for the two of you, but my first feeling was pain at our estrangement. Ella looked so totally content, your daughter was tiny and perfect, and I was miles away, not part of the picture.

My senior year in college, I took a psychology class where we learned that our personalities are not stable, that what we think we know about the people closest to us is sort of an illusion. Not only do people change over time, but often, our friends and family seem predictable only because we usually see them in familiar roles and situations. A father who is kind and helpful at home might be abusive at work; a teacher who is animated in the classroom might seem shockingly quiet when a student runs into her at the dog park. Over time, a person might learn to interpret events more positively and begin to react more positively; or, a person might suffer a trauma that fundamentally alters who they think they are. "Our personalities are always in flux," our professor said. Change itself is the only constant.

At the time, I didn't like this theory, which gave me the same swirling feeling I'd had as a child, staring out my window at night when I couldn't sleep, thinking about infinity. If my professor was right, it meant I could count on no one, not even myself. I couldn't predict the future or how I'd feel about it, and, therefore, didn't know who I'd be. I didn't like thinking this way.

Lately, though, I've found this theory comforting. The "me" I am now is not the final version but the person who exists at this moment, in this set of circumstances. My future self might be delightful. I think about all of the things that might happen to bring me and Ella back together. I also think of the times when people I know have acted out of character and replay them in my mind as proof that anything is possible. The time when my mild-mannered Republican grandmother stopped the car on the way home from the farmers' market to throw a tomato at an anti-abortion protester harassing women at a clinic. The time when my you-will-honor-your-obligations dad let me quit softball mid-season. The time when normally calm and compliant Ella fell off the monkey bars in kindergarten, broke her arm, and fled the nurse's office to run upstairs to the fourth-grade classrooms, shouting my name. She wasn't going anywhere without me, she screamed. She needed me and knew exactly where I was—the second classroom on the right, the room with the picture of the solar system on the door. We were taking a math test, but when I heard her voice, I left the paper on my desk and went to my sister, rocked her in my arms. "I've got you." I told her. "I'm always going to be right there." You can tell her, no matter what happens, I still mean it.

—*Caroline*

CHINCOTEAGUE

Nora hated driving to begin with—especially highway driving, especially with a car full of teenagers—and that day it was raining. Not hard enough to delay the trip, just opaque gray skies and slick roads, a steady thrum of raindrops that made half the drivers slow down and the other half swerve impatiently. Already they'd passed two accidents. When she saw the first sign for the Chesapeake Bay Bridge, she turned off her daughter Chloe's atmospheric house music and announced everyone would need to stop talking until they'd safely made it to the other side.

"Seriously?" Chloe said from the passenger seat. "Just pull over. I'll drive."

In the rearview mirror she could see her son and his ex-girlfriend Ruth smiling at each other. Around her he almost seemed like himself again, which was such a gift that Nora didn't care what Chloe had to say about the unfairness of Ruth being here. While Evan was withdrawing from his friends and ignoring his homework, Chloe was away at college. She didn't see him lose weight or quit the lacrosse team or become afraid of sleep. At night he would start out in his own bed but by morning she'd find him in the living room with the lights on, his laptop open, a message from Netflix asking if he was still watching, and he'd missed enough assignments that he might not graduate from high school in June. She and Brendan had been so worried he would hurt himself.

"Your life shouldn't be this stressful," Chloe said. "You should get medicated."

Nora started to say something but let it go. Chloe had a point—Nora's anxiety had skyrocketed lately—whose hadn't?—but this particular swinging bridge with its narrow lanes, no shoulders, and low railings made the gray water below them feel menacing. A digital sign at the entrance warned of a wind advisory.

"Okay, honey," she said. "Thanks for your feedback."

On sunny days, the bay sparkled, but today the water was a dull gray line on the edge of her vision that almost blended into the sky. At the height of the bridge, the wind shook the car. Nora kept her eyes on the road, made herself breathe, and eventually they were on the other side. She had a cramp in her right thigh and took one of the first exits, pulling into the parking lot of a local park with a playground, athletic fields, and a couple of picnic tables.

"I need to stretch my legs," she said. "Does anyone need the curtain?"

It was May 2020, and the curtain was a hot pink privacy tent she'd found on Amazon along with a camping toilet and set of disposable bags—their strategy for traveling responsibly during a pandemic. The curtain and the trip had been her husband's idea, but at the last minute, he'd had to cover for another oncologist and so now she was stuck with the driving and the pee bags and Chloe's bad attitude. She didn't blame him, though, if she'd known she'd be doing this alone, she would not have agreed to the trip. Plus, it was cooler than she'd expected it would be on Memorial Day weekend.

"No thanks," Chloe said. "I'll pee in the woods."

Nora, Ruth, and Evan huddled under a picnic shelter while Chloe walked toward a patch of skinny trees, pushing back brambles and vines. A couple of months ago, after William & Mary closed, she asked if her "friend" Emily could live with them in DC, and Nora and Brendan said no: He was working with immunosuppressed patients and needed to be careful, their DC townhouse was tiny, and Evan was still in the midst of a very hard time.

"Isn't everyone?" Chloe had said and accused them of discriminating against Emily who identified as nonbinary.

"Give me a break," Nora had said, but Chloe remained unconvinced.

Now Emily, who didn't get along with their parents, was living in a hotel in Williamsburg and working at Food Lion. Because of their exposure at the grocery store, Brendan and Nora had said Emily was welcome on this vacation but would need to stay outdoors.

"It's completely hypocritical," Chloe had said. "But I can't say I'm surprised. When it comes to me and Evan, you've never been fair."

Brendan assured Nora that Chloe was manipulating them, saying the thing she knew would get to them, but Nora was having trouble letting this remark go. Until recently, Evan had always been the easier, happier child, and maybe, her relief in having one carefree, amiable child had made Chloe think she loved him more.

When Chloe came back to the parking lot, Ruth walked toward the woods, and Nora waved Chloe over to the picnic shelter. Her intention was to call a truce, to tell her daughter how much she loved her, but when Chloe arrived scrolling on her phone, half-heartedly scowling up at Nora, she snapped, "Can you put the phone away? I want to talk to you and Evan." Chloe gave her a look but dropped the phone into her raincoat pocket. "Jesus, are you okay?"

"Let's have a good trip," she said. "Dad can't be here, and it's raining, but we're still very lucky. We're healthy and together. We have enough money to rent a vacation home—"

"Got it, Mom," Chloe said. "I'm totally spoiled and ungrateful. I know."

/ / / / / / /

The rental home was a small tan two-story house with aqua trim a few rows back from an inlet of water. It had a weathered roof, a screened-in porch, and a loose railing on the front steps. When they stepped inside, it was obvious the house was used only as a rental property. Dated or cheap furniture, plastic dishes and Formica countertops, a giant amateur painting of a mallard that hung over the mantel. The whole place smelled damp.

"Not great," she said. "But it's what was available."

Her kids ignored her, but Ruth hung back.

"I think it's okay," she said. "It's close to the national park, right? That's what we came to see anyway."

She had always liked Ruth who was skinny and freckled, self-possessed and kind. Before she'd ever met the girl, back when she couldn't have been more than about ten, she sent Nora and the rest of the school's board of directors a thank you note for expanding tuition remission to include the school's support staff like her mother who was an office administrator in the lower school. *I do not know what the future holds* the note read *but I have a feeling this school will change my life.*

Ruth was a fellow cross-country runner a year behind Evan and they'd dated throughout his sophomore and junior year. They went to prom together, lifted weights together, did homework side by side at Nora's dining-room table. They seemed so effortlessly happy that Nora would not have been surprised if they'd stayed together in college and eventually gotten married. When they'd suddenly broken up this past fall, Nora had felt heartbroken and confused. A few months later, when Evan told them his English teacher, Ms. Caldwell, had been abusing him, the breakup made sense: Ruth was one more thing that woman had stolen from her child.

Evan was the one who'd asked to bring Ruth on the trip, but when Ruth said no, Nora, unbeknownst to her son or husband, drove to her apartment complex in Bethesda and convinced her to go. She was, she knew, no better than those high-strung, hated-by-everyone Hollywood parents who had been involved in the college admissions scandal, a so-called "snowplow parent," but what were you supposed to do when your child was drowning and you saw one small way you might help?

Ruth answered the door with a confused and panicked look on her face that only got worse once Nora explained why she'd come.

"I don't know Ms. King," she'd said and stepped out onto the sidewalk. "I'm still not over him dumping me, and my parents are kind of strict about sleepovers with boys."

Ruth sounded certain, but she was wearing a Georgetown Baseball T-shirt that had once belonged to Evan, and she took this to be a sign that Ruth still cared.

"He's struggling," Nora said. "I'm not sure how much he's told you."

Ruth shook her head. She knew she had to tread lightly. Evan would not be happy she was here at all, but if she told Ruth anything about Ms. Caldwell, he wouldn't forgive her.

"Everything that happened this year has hit him really hard," she said carefully. "I know it's not fair to ask, but he could use a friend."

Ruth squinted at her and what seemed to be a look of realization passed over her face.

"I'll ask my parents," she said finally. "I'll let you know what they say."

Nora shook her head. "Just tell Evan. I wasn't here."

She promised Ruth's parents the room she shared with Evan would have two single beds, but when they all went upstairs to check out the house, they discovered the room only had a king.

"I thought—" Ruth said, looking at the bed.

Nora knelt down on the carpet to look under the mattress. "We'll fix it. I'm sure they come apart. See? It's two single beds hooked together."

They got the beds separated but after searching all the closets in the house, they couldn't find any sheets. She suggested they put in a Target order, but the closest store was an hour away.

It wasn't until she asked if Chloe would share a bed with her brother that Chloe admitted she'd brought an extra set of sheets for the following night when she and Emily would sleep on an air mattress inside a tent.

"Chloe!"

"What? I don't want to sleep on dirty sheets."

For dinner they ate the baked ziti she prepped ahead of time, whole wheat focaccia from an artisanal bakery, a Greek salad with kalamata olives and peperoncinis. For dessert she set out a plate of lemon bars, peanut butter blossoms, and those chewy chocolate caramel cookies she usually only baked at Christmas.

"Happy vacation," she said, clinking her wineglass with their water glasses, hoping the cheerfulness in her voice didn't sound desperate.

For months Evan had barely seemed to function. He played video games for hours, showered only when she nagged him. A couple weeks ago they'd had a meeting with his advising team who warned his admission to Northeastern could be revoked if his spring semester grades didn't improve, and he'd barely seemed to register the news. A year ago, they would have taken away his phone and his computer, made him sit with them each night to do his homework, but punishing him for being depressed felt cruel.

As soon as the call ended, she told Evan that if he ended up taking a year off or starting at a community college, this was okay, and he'd made a scoffing sound and slammed his belongings into his backpack.

"Expect more from me," he shouted. "Stop staring at me all the time like you feel sorry for me."

Nora didn't want to stare at Evan, but she wasn't sure how else she was supposed to know how he was doing. When Chloe was upset, she was loud and emotional, but Evan retreated and said nothing.

He might never have told them about Ms. Caldwell in the first place except he'd wanted to drop his journalism class, and they wouldn't let him. She'd been Chloe's adviser and favorite teacher, a pretty thirty-something who'd published two books of poetry and who was known for her no-nonsense attitude and challenging classes. They'd thought Evan wanted an easier teacher, and he said they didn't understand.

"It's not about the work," he said. "It's her. She's terrorizing me."

"What?" Nora asked. "What are you talking about?"

"She's a *horrible* person," Evan said. "You have no idea what she's capable of."

Brendan heard something that Nora didn't and put his hand on Evan's knee. "Did something happen?" he asked. "Did she hurt you?"

Eventually the story came out in bits and pieces. One afternoon, in the journalism lab, Ms. Caldwell had started touching his shoulders. When things got "out of hand," Evan froze. He'd never had a crush on her, he told them, but he hadn't said no. Soon they were meeting more often, and she was telling him she loved him, that she wanted to leave her husband. When he told her he couldn't do it anymore—he was having panic attacks—she told him he didn't have a choice. Every day, often multiple times each day, Nora fantasized about drowning the woman or throwing her in front of a train.

Ms. Caldwell had been put on unpaid leave immediately and soon fired. The headmaster had also sent an email to the school and alumni list explaining she'd been fired for having a sexual relationship with a student, and the story had been picked up by the local media. It was unlikely she'd teach again, but because Evan had been eighteen, the police wouldn't press charges.

After dinner, Ruth and Evan volunteered to do the dishes. Chloe disappeared upstairs, and Nora went to the bedroom just off the kitchen and started to unpack. Behind the door she could still hear Ruth and Evan talking about their classmates and the weirdness of Zoom school, which Tupperware containers and bowls they'd brought from home and which belonged to the rental. Then she heard Evan say in a low voice, "I was stupid to break up with you. It's honestly the biggest mistake of my life."

The water went on and off. A dish clanked in the rack.

"I know," Ruth said. "And if you break my heart again, I'm going to kick your ass."

/ / / / / / /

According to a couple online reviews, the wild ponies could be seen from an overlook on the park's Woodland Trail in the early mornings, and so Nora woke up before dawn to make four egg and cheese sandwiches and wrap them up in foil. She shuffled everyone out of the house just as the sun was rising, deep pinks and yellows backlighting the clouds.

"Gorgeous," she said, her coffee kicking in, her mind relaxed now that she was driving on a two-lane road in a town where everyone crept forward at twenty miles per hour. "I'm so grateful for the sunrise and that all of you are here with me to see it."

They crossed the salt marsh that separated the island where they were staying from the one that was home to the national park. She was thinking about how she used to make them all name something they were grateful for each night at the dinner table, how she used to be convinced this would help her privileged kids gain some perspective. She stopped herself from forcing them to do this ritual now, but Evan seemed to read her mind.

"I'm grateful my mom woke me up at the ass crack of dawn," he said. "I'm grateful Chloe isn't in charge of the music."

"Ha ha," Nora said sarcastically, though she was thrilled to hear him joking and happy she'd convinced Ruth to come. "Good one."

The trail was a paved loop lined with dead white tree skeletons stripped of their leaves and bark. The air smelled of pine, and they could hear birdsong and the ocean's waves in the distance. After about a half mile, they reached a wooden observation deck, where a gray-haired couple in Harley-Davidson windbreakers stared at their masked group skeptically. In the distance, four horses were visible, but even with binoculars, they were just blobs of color grazing.

"I thought they'd be closer," Nora said. "I can barely see them."

Online there had been dozens of pictures of these squat wild ponies running on the beach, tails whipping in the wind, but these animals in the field were far away and practically motionless. They'd had a better look at the penned ponies they'd seen outside the hotels getting photographed and fed handfuls of corn by tourists.

The man raised his chin in her direction. "The big herd is on the other side of the island," he said. "If you want to see more of them, you've got to go by boat."

"Ah, okay," Nora said. "Thanks."

She had read a little bit about the island and the wild ponies but hadn't done the usual legwork required to plan a good trip. Usually she ordered guidebooks, scoured online message boards for off-the-tourist-track beaches and restaurants, but in a normal year, they would go to France or Italy, Hawaii or Colorado. In the fifteen years they'd lived in DC, they'd never once vacationed in Maryland or Virginia, but they'd needed to go somewhere within driving distance and coming to the beach with the wild ponies she'd read about as a girl had felt romantic and freeing, an antidote to their months of constricted movements.

"Sorry I woke you up for this," she said, once the couple was out of earshot. "I'll see if I can book a boat ride for tomorrow."

Evan shrugged. "It's okay, Mom. Nobody cares about the ponies."

They followed the paved road to a dirt trail packed with crushed oyster shells and eventually reached an inlet of blue water. Yesterday's storm had passed, and the sun was out, but the air was still cool enough for a light jacket. They walked along the water's edge, and when they saw a strange-looking metal structure on a wooden platform, Evan and Ruth ran ahead to investigate. Chloe looked at a flock of gulls with her binoculars, and Nora took out the trail map and pretended that she wasn't watching Evan and Ruth, trying to figure out if they were falling back in love.

Chloe checked her phone and a look of anguish washed over her face. Nora suspected Emily had texted to say they couldn't make it, but it turned out to be Chloe's internship in Provincetown, which had been canceled.

"I should have known, but I was just hoping," she said. "It was the last good thing that might happen for a while."

The internship was at a writer's retreat where she would have done twenty hours of janitorial work each week in exchange for free lectures and poetry workshops. She would have needed to get a job at a restaurant to pay for her food and housing, and the internship itself seemed to have little practical use, but Nora knew this wasn't the point. What Chloe wanted was a summer in a sunlit seaside town filled with rainbow flags and queer people. In high school, she had announced she was pansexual and spent most of her time hanging around with kids she knew from Pride Club, some of whom had serious mental health issues. Chloe had dated two people that they knew of—a nice enough girl named Alex who wore gold aviator glasses and took photography classes and a sweet but troubled trans guy named Conrad who had been hospitalized twice for self-harm. Nora was fine with Chloe's sexuality—she'd always assumed she was queer; they'd picked this school because it was progressive—but she didn't love the fact that several of her friends seemed to be in a constant state of emotional distress. They were in and out of mental health treatments, struggling in school, fighting with their seemingly supportive parents, and often their depression felt contagious. After Conrad's first hospitalization, Chloe had become moody and fragile and had eventually started taking antidepressants. Nora was not proud to admit that when she'd first heard about Emily—a nonbinary kid at odds with their family—her first thought had been, "Jesus Christ, Chloe. Not again."

"Who knows if it will even be an option next summer either," Chloe said. "By then I'll need a real internship."

Nora thought Chloe was being dramatic: Everyone's summer had been canceled—some people had lost jobs, watched relatives die. But Nora knew it wouldn't be helpful to say so. Instead, she tried to, as her therapist had instructed, "reflect her child's emotions."

"You must be so disappointed," she said, tentatively resting her arm across Chloe's shoulder. "It was going to be such a good summer for you."

"Yeah," Chloe said. "It was."

They drove to the ocean side of the island, which was windy but bright, and walked along the sand, collecting shells. When they passed a stoic young woman in a fur coat and hat, Evan and Ruth cracked each other up by referring to the woman as Melania. After a while, Chloe and Nora set out a beach blanket and watched the water, and Evan and Ruth ran with the tide, in and out, letting the cold water chase them.

"He's so dumb. He acts like a little kid," Chloe said, but her voice was affectionate. To Nora, Evan and Ruth looked like puppies, frolicking.

Back at the rental, she moved the sheets to the drier, set out the overpriced brie, crackers, candied pecans, and shortbread cookies she'd splurged on for the trip, and they took turns using the showers. Nora went last and let herself take a long bath. By the time she dried her hair and came downstairs, Emily had arrived and was with Chloe, masked, turning kabobs on the grill. Someone had set out placements and silverware on the glass patio table.

"This is great," she said. "Thank you. I'm Nora by the way. It's nice to meet you."

Emily gave a little wave. "Emily. Thanks for having me. It's nice to meet you, too."

They had thick, wavy brown hair cut into a shag and were wearing a cropped floral top with loose high-waisted jeans, hot pink eyeshadow at the corners of their eyes. Nora didn't quite understand what it meant to be nonbinary if you went by a girl's name and wore pink, but Emily seemed friendly and helpful, and she appreciated that they were wearing a mask.

"What can I do?"

"Nothing," Chloe said. "You already prepped everything. Just relax."

While Chloe went inside to make a salad, Nora sat at the table and asked how Emily had been holding up. They talked about Food Lion, where coworkers kept getting sick and customers no longer made small talk, the strangeness of being in Williamsburg without students or tourists or the colonial actors you used to see sometimes walking around. Their life sounded difficult, but she didn't sense any of the resentment Chloe had about their current circumstances. Nora felt like an asshole for assuming Emily was depressed and a bigger asshole for having wanted to protect her daughter more than she'd wanted to help a young adult without a place to go.

"I can't believe this is how college ends," Emily said. "None of it feels real."

"What's next for you? Never mind. I'm sure that's a horrible question."

Emily shrugged. "It's okay. I have some interviews. I actually got a job offer with Northrop Grumman, but I have to think about it."

Nora tried to hide her disbelief, but when Emily saw it, they just laughed.

"I know. I never thought I'd work for a defense contractor either, but the money is good, and I have student loans. Plus, I can't rely on my parents."

She felt another surge of guilt. "Listen," she said. "I'm sorry we couldn't invite you to live with us. My husband works with cancer patients, and we already had four of us living in a townhouse, but I know you were in a bad spot, and I'm sorry."

Emily looked a little perplexed. "Oh, I didn't expect you to take me in."

"If you get stuck, we're here, though," Nora said. "And congratulations. A steady job right now is no small thing."

The temperature had dropped, and it felt almost too cold to eat outside, maybe pointless anyway if Chloe was making out with Emily, but this was the agreement she and Brendan had made. The food was cold before they finished eating and to compensate, Nora offered them Pinot Noir—full glasses for Emily and Chloe and half glasses for Evan and Ruth.

"Why?" Evan said. "Yesterday you said no."

"It's chilly," Nora said. "I thought the wine might help."

After dinner, Chloe pointed out a firepit and woodpile Nora hadn't noticed and asked if they could make a fire.

"Sure," she said. "Why not?"

Emily and Chloe arranged the logs and fanned the flames with a cereal box while Ruth and Evan moved plastic lawn chairs around in a circle. The lawn was low and wet in some places but there was a dome of elevated sand around the firepit. Once the fire was going strong, Emily sat by Chloe and put a hand on her knee. Ruth and Evan asked Emily questions about college and the world "out there" that they largely hadn't seen since March. They all talked about how boring it was to take classes online, how much they missed their friends, but the tone was upbeat, almost giddy. When Emily's hand moved higher on Chloe's leg, Nora announced that she was going to sleep and that since the lawn was so damp, Emily and Chloe should feel free to sleep on an air mattress on the screened-in porch instead of in the tent. This was a small gesture—the porch was old and they would still practically be outside—but Chloe seemed pleased.

Inside she found an extra comforter that she brought out to the porch and then poured herself another glass of wine and FaceTimed Brendan.

"Everybody's happy," she said. "Nobody's arguing. You should have seen Ruth and Evan chasing each other around the beach. He actually seems like himself."

Brendan smiled. His eyes were red, and he looked exhausted. "Good."

She was proud of herself for smoothing things over with Emily and Chloe and for knowing somehow that what Evan had needed was connection. She started to tell him about visiting Ruth but stopped herself.

"Thank you," she said instead. "I'm so glad you suggested this trip."

Nora woke up to the sound of the screen door slamming and Chloe swearing. It was past seven, but a headache throbbed in her right eye socket. She had almost gone back to sleep when she heard voices in the kitchen. At first, she thought it was Chloe and Emily—hopefully masked, hopefully just using the bathroom—but then she heard Ruth's voice.

"Do you think there's any way Emily could take me to a pharmacy?" she whispered.

"The only one that's opened on Sundays is thirty minutes away, but it's kind of an emergency."

Chloe said something Nora couldn't hear, and she grabbed the glass beside the bed, swallowed the stale water, and put it against the door to amplify the sound. She wasn't proud of herself, but she was the adult, and shouldn't she know what was happening? There was a long enough pause that Nora thought she'd missed the answer, but then Ruth said, "Um . . . Plan B?"

Nora's heart squeezed.

"I won't tell my mom or anything," Chloe said. "Don't worry."

Ruth laughed. "She gave me wine, and I'm pretty sure she had them put the twin beds together. I feel like she *wanted* us to hook up."

Nora couldn't breathe. This wasn't true. How could Ruth believe this was true? What she had wanted was the sweet relationship she and Evan had before Ms. Caldwell had ruined his life. What she had wanted was the opposite of this.

"Wow."

"If I tell you something, would you not tell Evan?"

"Okay?"

"She came to my house and kind of pressured me to come on this trip."

"Jesus Christ."

"It's whatever," Ruth said. "I'm not sorry about what happened. I'm the one who wanted to hook up. I just don't think your mom will care about this."

"She has no boundaries," Chloe whispered. "She acts like our privileges make us weak, but it's her. She can't stop herself from micromanaging our lives."

They were both quiet for a moment and then Ruth said, "What happened with Emily?"

"I have no idea. I thought things were fine, but apparently I came on too strong."

"That sucks."

Nora thought of the perplexed look on Emily's face when she'd mentioned their living situation and told herself not to overthink it—surely the breakup had nothing to do with her—but she felt a twinge of guilt anyway.

"It does, but it's also fine," Chloe said. "We're pretty different. It probably wasn't going to work out anyway."

Chloe sounded less upset than she would have expected, and Nora let herself zone out for a bit. She was thinking about the boat cruise she'd booked and now regretted, her headache, and also how much she needed to pee, when she heard Chloe confess that she'd texted Ms. Caldwell to tell her about her internship being canceled.

"I know I'm supposed to break off all contact, but I actually miss her," Chloe said. "Do you think it would be awful if I met up with her?"

Nora's blood pressure spiked so quickly that she felt dizzy, and it took all her restraint not to fling open the door and scream.

"I'm sorry," Ruth said eventually "but I think it's a bad idea. Evan is kind of traumatized. As far as I'm concerned, she's a rapist."

Chloe mumbled something she couldn't hear and then apologized.

"You're right," she said. "I don't know why I miss her so much."

"You're not, like, in love with her, are you?"

She couldn't hear an answer, but Nora knew immediately that Ruth was right.

She waited as long as she could to leave the room and pee and then took a long hot shower. She made eggs and pancakes in almost total silence, but no one seemed to notice. When Chloe said she needed to drive to another town to get a phone charger for Ruth, she seemed poised for an argument, but Nora handed over the keys.

"Wow, okay," Chloe said, staring at her. "Thanks."

"Just go," Nora said. "If you wait around, I'll change my mind."

/ / / / / / /

The boat cruise was fifty-five dollars per person for a two-hour ride narrated by a heavyset retired naval officer named "Captain Jerry." Out on the water, it was windy and cold. Every few minutes, the boat idled so that Captain Jerry could point to distant wildlife and deliver commentary filtered through a conservative lens. He was opposed to oversight by the Fish and Wildlife Commission and believed the volunteer fire department that owned the ponies on the Virginia side of the island should not have to pay taxes on the land they used. On the Maryland side of the island, the National Park Service controlled the population with birth control darts, and Captain Jerry seemed opposed both to the birth control and the National Park Service.

"Their story is that the horses came from settlers," he said. "But the genetic tests they've run can tell you that doesn't hold water."

The story he preferred was a Spanish shipwreck that happened before the arrival of English settlers, the marooned horses fleeing to shore, somehow finding a way to survive.

Chloe, who was on the bench beside her, took pictures with her phone. Ruth and Evan sat on the other side of the aisle, huddled under a blanket borrowed from the tour company. When Captain Jerry began to talk about the social dynamics of the so-called harem bands of mares who "belong" to a single stallion, Ruth looked like she might throw up, but Nora knew she was probably just nauseated from the Plan B.

"Here we go!" Captain Jerry shouted. "This is Riptide's band, and as you can see, he likes the blonds."

He pointed to a chestnut-colored stallion in the distance, grazing in a field with several ponies with blond manes. According to Captain Jerry, these ponies had survived only because their bodies adapted over generations to the harsh conditions of their environment. They were squat and scruffy with bloated bellies and had thick stomachs and enlarged kidneys. When other breeds had been introduced to diversify the gene pool, they'd all died pretty quickly. It seemed to Nora that there was a lesson here about resilience and survival, but she couldn't say what the lesson was.

As soon as they stepped off the boat, Nora handed her car keys to Chloe.

"My head hurts," she said. "Just be careful."

She cranked up the heat and watched the RV parks and vacation homes slide by. She was overwhelmed, tired, not sure what to think. Should she be happy Ruth had the maturity to get herself to a pharmacy, or was this just what it felt like—another parenting failure, another lapse in judgment from one of her kids? She was furious with Chloe for contacting Ms. Caldwell but felt compassion for her, too. What had it felt like to discover her mentor, who she had apparently also loved, had come for her brother? Back when Chloe was in ninth grade, the Parents' Association at her kids' school had sponsored a lecture by a parenting expert who argued that their goal as parents should not be to prevent their children from failing but to raise self-sufficient kids. At the time, she'd laughed at the stories of parents cutting up steak for their twelve-year-olds and making their kids' science fair projects. She was thinking about how sure she'd been that she was different, how little she'd known then about how high the stakes could feel, when she heard Chloe scream and felt the car lurch as she slammed on the brakes.

"Oh my God," Chloe shrieked. "Jesus Christ."

When Nora looked up, a pony stood feet in front of the SUV— brown and white spotted with a black mane. Up close, he looked wild and strange—a ragged coat, bumpy with mud and scars, a thick muscular body, a dark wet mouth chewing a long amber reed.

Chloe was shaking. "He ran into the road out of nowhere. I thought I was going to kill him."

At the roundabout ahead of them, a police barricade blocked traffic, and Nora saw that it was not just this pony but a whole group that had made its way into town. Three ponies grazed in the grass by a Days Inn; another one had stopped in the middle of the road. A small group of people had gathered in the parking lot of the Days Inn to watch.

"Can we get out?" Evan asked.

Nora nodded. "Just not too close."

When Chloe opened the door, the spotted pony darted across the road and pranced through the soggy grass in front of a pink cottage advertising vacation rentals. Ahead of them a police officer directed traffic. In the parking lot of the Days Inn, they watched the ponies shake flies and eat grass. Ruth took a video. People came out of hotel rooms, more cars stopped, and a crowd began to form. The mood in the air was one of wonder and excitement, though she was disappointed to hear that these were likely not *really* wild ponies but rather that some of the penned ponies on display for tourists had probably escaped.

When a little girl in pigtails walked right up to a pony, Nora expected a parent to stop her, but no one did. The girl, who looked about five or six, pet his tail and then reached up to touch his face, at which point, the pony flicked back his ears and shook his head.

A man called out, "You want to give him some space now," but the girl stayed still. Nora's heart lurched. The girl could be bit, kicked, trampled, but she just stood in the spooked horse's path, unmoving.

"Lindy!" a woman yelled. "Move back."

The woman had long, damp hair and was wearing a tracksuit and Nike slides. She handed the toddler on her hip to what looked like a stranger. She ran toward her daughter, but the pony reacted first, shaking his mane and throwing his feet in the air, just missing the girl's head before he galloped off toward a patch of grass by the dumpsters.

Her mother picked her up and the little girl threw her arms around her, sobbing. As her children wandered away, Nora watched the woman and her daughter. She could feel the girl's weight and her grip, the woman's heart and breath slowly resetting their pace.

HAPPINESS

I moved in with Angela after five months because her roommate was moving to California and because I was sick with love. I was twenty-five, and this had never happened to me. Before Angela, I'd dated only men—and "dated" is kind of an exaggeration. I'd hung out with each guy long enough to prove I *could* have a boyfriend, sometimes had sex with him, and then immediately informed him it was not going to work out. My longest relationship had lasted seven weeks.

But that spring in Arizona, with a nearly perfect season of blue skies, sunlight, and long breezy days when green spaces filled with frisbees and sunbathers and the restaurant patios overflowed with diners, a feeling of possibility hung in the air. My life finally seemed to be coming together.

"It's just a sublease," Angela said. "And just for a few months. If things fall apart, you'll have a way out."

I did not want a way out. I wanted to stitch my life to hers, and living together seemed like a good first step. What I said, though, was "Sure. My lease is almost up. Why not?"

We were at my apartment in the shower, a mildewed plastic stall that made a popping sound when you shifted your weight. There wasn't enough space for us both to be under the showerhead, so we took turns shivering against the wall.

"What a cliché, right?" she said, meaning how quickly we were moving in together.

"Totally," I said. I had learned the joke only a couple of weeks earlier when we were watching *The L Word*: What does a lesbian bring to a second date? A U-Haul.

I had graduated from Arizona State with a degree in trumpet performance and hadn't yet found a reason to leave Tempe. Because I'd gone to college on a music scholarship, I had genuinely thought I'd land a job in a major orchestra after graduation. When this didn't happen, I found myself working at House of Tricks, the same cozy "new American" restaurant where I'd worked in college, and as a cashier at the Buffalo Exchange. I actually loved both jobs, which involved long periods of standing around and gossiping about my coworkers' sex lives, but my lack of progress toward adulthood shamed me. My friend Serena was about to graduate from Berkeley Law, and my high school friend Jenny was already married.

The only cool thing about me was that I played trumpet in a band called the Tree Frogs. Our festive mix of mariachi horns and reggae beats was popular at local bars, even though we were not very good. The other band members were mostly guys from the restaurant who'd taught themselves just enough about music to attract women and not so much that our performances were consistently in tune. What people liked about us, I think, was the energy of a half dozen people on stage dancing to a thumping mix of brass, tambourines, and strings. What I liked was how the band transformed me from a quiet, self-conscious person into a woman who stomped around in short dresses and tall boots, swinging the bell of her trumpet like she was in a New Orleans marching band. This alter ego was what made Angela notice me.

"You looked like such a badass up there," she told me at the bar after a performance. "I loved watching you."

"That's why I dress like this," I told her. "I'm glad to see it worked."

My whole body tingled in her presence. She was wearing tight jeans and a ribbed tank top that showed off her slender arms and a tattoo of birds taking flight. She had almost-black hair, long eyelashes, and a masculine swagger that made my stomach flutter. This, I realized, was who I'd been waiting to find me.

"This is the third time I've meant to talk to you," she said. "You make me so shy."

I felt a dizzy, floating sensation as the sweat from the stage cooled on my skin. If I could just keep it together, I thought, my life was about to change.

/ / / / / / /

Angela was only two years older than I was but had already been working as a middle-school math teacher for five years—first in California, where she was from, and then in Tempe, where she had moved to be closer to her brother, Diego, and his family. She had curtains on her windows and a plan to buy a house before she turned thirty. When I moved in, all of my belongings fit into the back of her brother's pickup truck.

"You travel light," he said.

Diego's pale brown eyes always flickered as if he was about to tell a joke. There wasn't any judgment in his voice, but I felt myself blushing. Angela said something to him in Spanish that I didn't understand beyond the word *she*.

"I told him you were a free spirit," she said and squeezed my hand. "Isn't that right?"

Free was the opposite of what I felt. Immobilized would have been more accurate.

Her place was a beige two-bedroom stucco house about ten minutes south of the university, in a neighborhood of more small beige houses sandwiched between some railroad tracks and a middle school.

The area was mostly occupied by students and young, broke families who left plastic toys in their yards, but to me it represented real adulthood. Before that I'd lived in a sprawling apartment complex where someone had once stolen my underwear from the dryer and before that a dorm room decorated with a giant Miles Davis poster and before that my childhood bedroom with the glow-in-the-dark plastic stars stuck to the ceiling. Angela's house had a fenced-in backyard with a lemon tree and a front porch where we drank coffee in the mornings and vodka sodas on the weekends.

Without roommates, we walked around naked and had sex wherever we wanted. Almost as intoxicating, though, was the easy domestic routine—cooking pasta while listening to music, making a grocery list, even mopping the terra-cotta floors. In the mornings she got up first, and I lay in the bed and watched her get dressed, wondering at my good fortune. Was it possible that fixing my life could be this simple?

For weeks I waited for the cracks in our relationship to show, and when they finally did, it was almost a relief. I was at the restaurant, finishing up a lunch shift, when Angela texted to say she'd be home early and her four-year-old nephew, Jaxon, would be with her. He'd gotten sent home from day care with a fever, and his parents were at work and couldn't get him.

I texted back, *Aren't YOU working?*

Yeah, but it's fine.

Angela was a more generous person than I was. She picked friends up at the airport at odd hours, had people over for drinks or dinner who never reciprocated. But leaving work early so her brother wouldn't have to felt like a different level of sacrifice, and it made me anxious. As a teenager, my parents' strict rules had so thoroughly controlled my behavior and sense of self that I'd spent my life since then keeping people at a distance. I didn't know how to navigate the give-and-take of close relationships without losing my sense of self, and Angela's attitude of accommodation felt threatening.

Just being protective of you, I texted back. *You are a giving person and people can take advantage.*

She didn't respond right away, and I had to close out my last table—a group of women from the neighborhood's mosque who'd been drinking tea and poking at a single slice of cake for approximately three hours. When I came back to the host stand, I had a series of messages waiting. *I wasn't asking for advice* was one. Also, *This is my family.*

I overstepped and I'm sorry, I texted, but she didn't respond. In the kitchen I wiped down the ketchup bottles and sugar boats and tried to tell myself that everything would be okay. I didn't want to lose her and have to go back to my old life. Chad, the bass player and lead singer in the Tree Frogs, was changing one of the syrups on the soda machine. He was a lanky white guy with floppy hair and an ironic handlebar mustache.

"What's wrong?" he asked. "Why does your face look like that?"

"I pissed off Angela."

"Don't do that." He threw the old syrup container across the room into the garbage can. "She's way too hot, Melanie. Don't fuck this up."

/ / / / / / /

When I got home, the blinds in the living room were closed and the DVR was playing an episode of *Brothers & Sisters* with the sound muted and the subtitles on. Angela was on the couch with Jaxon sprawled across her, half asleep. His cheeks were flushed, and his eyes looked heavy. Every other time I'd seen him, he was barreling across a playground or jumping on the furniture.

"Is he okay?" I asked. "Do you need me to go to the pharmacy or something?"

She kissed his caramel-colored curls. "He'll be all right. He just has a low fever."

"Are *we* okay?"

"Let's talk later."

In my past "relationships" I had often been accused of having no emotions. At first some guys saw this as a perk: I didn't care if he slept over after sex or kept in touch with his exes. But eventually it was said in anger, after I broke up with him.

"This is just an ego trip for you," one guy told me. "You make men fall in love with you just to bust their balls. There's something wrong with you."

His name was Keith, and we'd briefly dated the summer after college graduation. He was a short, well-dressed cello player who was in a music fraternity with many of my friends, and he had seen how I operated long enough to recite a whole list of men I had wronged. He was on the verge of tears, but I didn't feel sorry for him. As far as I could tell from my female friends, men did this to women all the time.

"Thanks for the insight," I said. "I'll keep that in mind."

Now, though, nauseated at the thought of Angela breaking up with me, I finally felt some sympathy for Keith and every other guy I'd dumped. I hadn't considered that they might have been telling the truth, that heartbreak could cause physical pain.

Angela and I had planned to go to an early movie with some of my friends, but when the time came to go, Diego still hadn't come to pick up Jaxon.

"Go without me," she said. "It's okay."

I was annoyed but wanted to mend things with her. "They'll understand," I said. "I'll stay and make dinner."

I made grilled cheese sandwiches and apple slices to appeal to Jaxon, but he didn't eat. Then the three of us watched *Planet Earth*, the one kid-appropriate DVD we had, while we waited for Diego. He knocked on the door a little before seven o'clock, grateful but not apologetic. Angela told him she was happy to help.

"He's my little guy," she said. "You know you can always call me."

When we were finally alone, I asked if she was still mad.

"This isn't about being mad. It's about compatibility. My family is everything to me. I can't be with somebody who doesn't understand that."

"Okay."

"Also, I had a free period at the end of the day. I'm not an idiot."

"I know that," I said. "I'm sorry. Please don't break up with me."

She sighed. "I'm making sure we're on the same page. If my brother needs me, I don't want to argue about it."

I said I understood.

"I come from a big Mexican family. This is who I am."

I thought, but did not say, that this wasn't the whole story. Her parents had married young, and her mom, who was white and used drugs, would disappear for months at a time. Once, when Angela was in elementary school, her mom passed out in the bathroom and she and her brother held a mirror under her nose to see if she was still breathing. When she was in middle school, her mom sold a leather jacket Angela had saved up to buy. Most of the time, though, Angela's mom was gone entirely, and her dad was often working or tired. Meanwhile I had grown up under the watchful eye of anxious and orderly Midwesterners who believed that good people shoveled their snow immediately and went to church each Sunday and forbade "slutty" clothing such as leggings and tank tops. I'd felt so scrutinized and controlled growing up that my parents' opinions still sometimes drowned out my own.

"I *like* who you are," I said, suddenly choked up. "Actually I love you, Angela."

It was the first time I'd said this to someone I was dating, and I was immediately afraid she wouldn't say it back.

"Well, I love you, too, Melanie," she said and then grinned. "Just don't come between me and my family."

/ / / / / /

June in Tempe was hot yet bearable, but by July you could feel your skin and hair burning as soon as you stepped outside. It wasn't possible to eat or exercise outdoors for most of the day, plastic grocery bags melted in cars, and the air shimmered with heat. The previous two summers I'd spent a couple of weeks at my parents' house in Missouri, where the heat was only mildly intolerable, and I could enjoy their air-conditioning and eat their sloppy joe sandwiches and green bean casserole for free. Each visit we would have at least one argument about my bad manners and ingratitude, but while they were at work, I could be alone in an empty house not tainted by my bad moods and loneliness. The summer I lived with Angela, though, I didn't visit my parents. When I told my mom that I might not be coming home at all before Christmas, she offered to buy me a plane ticket.

"It's not that," I said. "I'm just busy with music, and I'm too old to take your money."

My mom seemed confused; I had never objected to their paying for things. But, I hadn't yet come out to her or mentioned Angela.

"Don't you at least want to come with us to the lake? Ben is coming."

Ben was my twenty-two-year-old brother who I hadn't been close to in about a decade. The lake was a murky, foul-smelling reservoir slick with oil from speedboats. My grandparents owned a musty cabin there the size of a storage shed, which my mom always remembered as large and inviting.

"It sounds nice," I said. "I wish I weren't so busy."

I was not busy. The restaurant was closed for the whole month of July, and the Tree Frogs were on hiatus until our lead singer finished his legal internship in Chicago. I worked about twenty hours a week at the Buffalo Exchange, but with most of the college students out of town for the summer, business was slow, and I often got sent home early, which was fine with me, even though my savings were dwindling. Now that she was on her summer break, Angela was more relaxed, more likely to have a drink during the week, and more willing to have loud sex in the middle of the day. Also I just liked being in her presence. I'd never reached the stage of dating where I bore witness to someone's daily life, and everything about her fascinated me. She loved sugar but drank her coffee black. She liked mystery novels and wore eyeliner every day, even if it was just the two of us. She was rarely idle, always working through a list of summer projects, from revising her curriculum to organizing her closets. She also volunteered several days a week to take care of Jaxon, which she genuinely seemed to enjoy.

His parents had taken him out of day care for the summer to save money. Usually his great-grandmother watched him during the day, but she was old and often needed a break. I was surprised to find that I liked having Jaxon around. We made slime from baking soda and school glue, took him to story hour at the library, brought him along with us while we ran errands. I was amazed at how good it felt when he reached for my hand and how friendly the world became when you walked through it with a child. Grizzled old men at Home Depot stopped to wave at him. Women at Safeway told Angela what an adorable little boy she was raising. Who they thought I was in this scenario wasn't clear. Neighbors we'd seen but never spoken to suddenly stepped out of the background to introduce themselves.

One morning, just after Jaxon's mom had dropped him off, we were on the sidewalk, trying to teach him to ride a bike Angela had found at a garage sale, when a little girl crossed the street to talk to us. She had a bike, too, but was older than Jaxon, maybe nine or ten, with tangled blond hair and a big purple T-shirt with a picture of a unicorn. I got the feeling she'd been waiting around for someone to talk to.

"I'm Kendra," she said.

"This is Jaxon," Angela said. "Jaxon, can you say hi?"

He looked up at the older girl as if she were a celebrity, but he didn't speak.

"I'm not allowed to talk to strangers unless they're ladies with kids," she said. "That's my mom's rule."

I gave Angela a look. I was pretty sure that, whatever ladies her mom had in mind, they probably weren't childless lesbians.

"Jaxon is actually my nephew," Angela said, "but I like your mom's idea about finding a family."

She followed us to the park and hung out while we watched Jaxon on the playground. When it was time for his morning snack, we headed back to our house. It seemed like Kendra wanted to come inside.

"I hope we see you around, Kendra," Angela said. "Do you live on this street?"

She nodded and pointed to a tiny cinder-block house with a blue door and an empty gravel driveway.

"Weird kid, right?" I said to Angela later. Kendra had seemed too eager for adult attention. Wasn't it dangerous for a little girl to broadcast such neediness?

"I don't know," Angela said. "I just got the feeling she was bored."

\ \ \ \ \ \ \

That summer I grew optimistic about my future. I'd learned that someone could fall in love with me, and I could love her back. With this weight lifted, everything else seemed possible. I paid off a parking ticket I'd been ignoring for six months and finally visited Arizona State's career center, which I'd been meaning to do for years. I began applying for sound-editing jobs at radio stations and ad agencies as well as entry-level sales and marketing positions that had nothing to do with music. I was going to be a different person now. I would no longer take money from my parents or watch marathons of *Desperate Housewives*. I would make my bed, pay my bills on time, eat three meals a day. From now on, even if Angela broke up with me, I was going to be an adult.

"My life is so much better with you," I tried to explain one night in bed, her head resting on my shoulder.

"I'm happy, too," she said and kissed my neck. "It was smart of me to find you."

But I knew she didn't understand. From what she'd told me, she had always been steady and capable, especially when her mom had left and her dad had needed her help around the house. Any instability in my own life had been self-inflicted.

During this slow, hot stretch of summer, strange, wide-eyed Kendra began to appear regularly in our lives. Whenever we left our house, she was there, looping around the cul-de-sac on her bike. Once, she rang our doorbell to ask for a glass of milk to make macaroni and cheese. Another time she came by to report that she'd fallen off her bike and scraped her knee. I was home alone, and I brought a folding chair out for her to sit on while I dug through the boxes in our hall closet to find Angela's first aid supplies. I knelt beside Kendra, dabbed a cotton ball soaked in hydrogen peroxide on her scraped knee, and covered the wound with ointment and bandages.

"There you go," I said, feeling as if I'd passed a test, but she just gave me a bland, satisfied look.

Perhaps because she worked with kids, Angela didn't seem to spend much time thinking about Kendra when she wasn't there, but I was flattered that the girl had attached herself to us and was eager to provide the kind of adult presence she needed.

During the summer Angela and I replaced the easy pasta or stir-fry dinners of the school year with the more time-consuming empanadas, pulled pork sandwiches, sourdough flatbread pizzas, and carne asada. We danced while we cooked and took turns playing DJ. She liked classic rock and country, while I favored singer-songwriters with whispery voices and acoustic guitars. She teased me that this was typical of kids whose older parents had made them listen to Bob Dylan instead of Michael Jackson. In fact, my parents had usually listened to silence, but I liked her theory anyway, because it suggested that my personality was not my fault.

One evening in late July the doorbell rang. It was Kendra.

"I'm locked out," she said. "Can I stay here until my mom gets home?"

I hesitated. It was a hot night, and she was probably hungry, but I didn't think we should be bringing someone else's child into our house, especially since we were gay. Prop 8 was on the ballot in California that fall, and we saw the bumper stickers in Arizona, too: the male + female stick-figure marriage equation, the "family values" slogans suggesting that gay people were harmful to kids.

"Hold on," I said, trying to sound casual.

When I relayed the situation to Angela in the kitchen, she shrugged and said we should call Kendra's mom. She ushered Kendra inside and pointed to the couch. "Do you know your mom's phone number? Does she have a cell phone?"

"She might not answer," Kendra said. "She's not allowed to at work."

I imagined her mom had some low-paying job with long, irregular hours. She was rarely home, even on the weekends. The handful of times I'd seen her ducking in and out of the house, she'd had on jean shorts and a T-shirt, her long blond ponytail looped through a baseball cap. If there was a dad in the picture, I never saw him.

Kendra's mom didn't answer, but Angela left a friendly message that included her name, address, and phone number. "It's fine for her to stay here until you're home," she said. "I just wanted you to know where she is." Then she asked Kendra, "Are you hungry? Do you like Mexican food?"

Kendra nodded and followed us to the kitchen.

We'd just sat down to eat when the phone rang. I heard Angela give a quick string of affirmative answers: "Yes," "okay," "sure, no problem."

"Your mom says she's on her way home," she told Kendra. "She wants you to wait for her at your house."

Kendra looked disappointed.

"Do you want to eat something first?"

She shook her head.

"What about a granola bar or something like that?"

"Maybe."

"Do you need to use our bathroom?"

"Yes."

While Kendra was in the bathroom, Angela got a granola bar and a package of fruit snacks from the supply she kept for Jaxon. As we walked Kendra to the front door, I felt as disappointed as she looked.

"We'll be here," I said, "if something comes up."

I stayed at the door and watched her walk across the street. Her neighbor's motion-sensor light clicked on and illuminated both lawns.

She sat down on her porch and opened the snacks, looking sad and resigned.

"I don't think her mom is on her way," I said.

"No," Angela said, "probably not."

That she had suspected this all along felt like a betrayal.

"She's *nine*," I reminded her.

"What do you want me to do? Her mom doesn't know us. We're strangers."

"Do you think a nine-year-old should be home alone every day?"

Angela's face tensed. "A lot of nine-year-olds are home alone. It's none of our business."

This didn't sound right to me. I didn't think Kendra was in danger necessarily, but I thought her mom was a bad parent, and I wanted Angela to agree.

"I think we have to do something."

Angela shook her head. "What are you going to do? Report her to Child Protective Services?"

It hadn't occurred to me, but it didn't sound like a bad idea. When I'd volunteered at a Jumpstart program in high school, we'd been told to share any suspicions we had. If there wasn't a problem, they assured us, nothing would happen.

"Maybe," I said. "If there's nothing wrong, they won't take her kid."

Angela gave a dismissive snort. "I hope you're joking."

When I didn't say anything, she asked if I'd ever reported someone.

"No."

She reminded me that, as a teacher, she was required to report signs of abuse or neglect to the authorities and that she worked with students for whom these signs were not uncommon. Even when children were seriously in danger, she said, it devastated them to be removed from their homes and risking that outcome, when it wasn't clear that Kendra was in danger, just to ease my own conscience was not okay.

"You're being selfish right now," she said. "It bothers me that you can't see that."

I was surprised by how angry she was, by her certainty that she was right. What if something happened to Kendra? What if she was in trouble and just waiting for someone to notice?

"I don't understand why you're so upset," I said. "You're acting kind of insane."

A flash of anger passed across her face. She took a breath to say something, then changed her mind.

"Do what you need to do," she said finally. "But if you call the police on this lady, I can't promise I'll forgive you."

Then she locked herself in our room. After about thirty minutes the door opened, and she tossed my pajamas and pillow into the hallway. I lay awake that night on my old twin mattress in the spare bedroom, watching rectangular shadows float across the ceiling. I had the feeling I was looking at my life from the outside, but I also felt strangely calm. Angela's reaction had felt so overblown that I knew it must be personal, and I was sure that I would wake up to another story about her mom and an apology.

The next morning, though, she didn't apologize, and when I asked if Kendra's mom reminded her of her own parents, she got angry. "This doesn't have anything to do with me," she said. "It's kind of insulting that you think that."

"I don't get it then," I said. "We don't even know this woman."

We were on the back porch drinking coffee and eating toast, watching a teal-green hummingbird flit around the hedges. Beyond the fence a riding lawn mower growled around the middle school. I was working the lunch shift at the restaurant, which had just reopened, but I didn't need to leave for a couple of hours. Angela was wearing sunglasses, and when she finally spoke, she lifted them up so I could see her eyes.

"I'm worried you're going to take this the wrong way."

I tensed up. "Okay."

"I think you've had a sheltered life," she said. "I feel like sometimes it makes you naive."

She was naming my worst secret. I *was* sheltered, and I didn't want to be that way. My heart was racing, and I could feel a security gate sliding down over my face.

"Let's pretend nothing's happening then," I said. "If I ignore the fact that this kid's loser mom abandons her every day, does that make me open-minded?"

She made a scoffing sound. "Wow, okay. I'm trying to *talk* to you, Melanie."

I understood this was an invitation to de-escalate, but I was too scared of what she would say next. I picked up my plate and coffee cup and brought them inside.

"Seriously, Melanie," I heard her say. "We have to be able to talk."

I rinsed my dishes and put them in the dishwasher. Then I got dressed and packed up my trumpet and sheet music and biked over to the practice rooms at Arizona State, which I knew would be unlocked and empty. I chose the room I'd reserved every day in my senior year: a narrow space with a small window and a black upright piano. I started with scales and warm-ups, an easy trumpet solo from a Tree Frogs song. Then I moved on to the Haydn Trumpet Concerto, which I'd memorized for a young artist competition in high school. Almost as soon as I began, it was obvious I was too rusty. My tone wasn't clear or consistent, and I could no longer reliably hit the high notes. I knew I could eventually get it back with weeks of serious practice, but I also knew that I wouldn't put in the time, and this brought a new adult kind of sadness: the conscious choice to leave something worse than it could be.

The restaurant wasn't very crowded, and some of my favorite coworkers were back, including a dark-haired hostess named Molly who studied architecture and had a tiny heart tattooed on the back of her ear. She'd once told me how she posed naked for art classes to make extra money, which made me view her with awe. When there was a lull, I brought a bag of unfolded table linens to the bench behind the host stand so I could get her advice about Angela.

"She's going to break up with me," I said. "I don't know what I'm going to do." Just admitting this out loud made me woozy.

"You're getting to know each other," Molly said. "Of course you're going to fight sometimes."

I shook my head. "She doesn't like who I am. You can't recover from that."

\ \ \ \ \ \ \

When I came home that afternoon, I apologized for running away and braced myself to listen to all of the bad things Angela had to say about me, but she was gentle. Other people's situations were different from mine, she said. She just wanted me to see that. She was sorry that she'd overreacted and locked herself in the bedroom.

"I'm sorry, too," I said, embarrassed that the person she was describing—blind to everyone's differences—sounded so much like my parents. "You're right. I'll work on it."

Soon after that, Angela went back for teacher workdays, and I started an unpaid internship at the Phoenix public radio station. Kendra all but disappeared, and I assumed that her mom had told her to stay away from us. I wondered if she was okay, if she missed us, if I'd been right not to report her mom. When I checked the mail, I lingered on the porch; when I walked home from work, I slowed passing by her house, hoping she might step outside and show me a new trick she'd learned on her bike. Sometimes I thought about knocking on the door and introducing myself to her mom, but she was rarely home, and what exactly would I say?

The relaxed summer gave way to a busy fall filled with minor disagreements. Every day Angela seemed to retreat a little more, and when she broke up with me in October, I was unsurprised but still shell-shocked.

Within a year I'd have an entry-level job at the radio station, and then, a few years later, a better job at a station in New York, where I would eventually meet my wife. But I didn't know this yet, and I was worried that, without Angela, I'd lose my tenuous grip on adulthood. When I asked her to reconsider, she didn't even seem to think about it.

"I'm sorry," she said. "I just don't see us together long-term."

In the last few weeks before I moved out, Angela avoided the house, and I was often home alone at night. I thought a lot about Kendra.

Then one night, a few days before I moved out, I was folding clothes on the couch when I saw a flash of movement at Kendra's house. It was just past dusk, the sky not totally drained of color, and the blinds were open to their living room. From where I was sitting, it looked like someone was getting chased. I grabbed my cell phone and keys, slid on my shoes, and went outside in a rush of concern and, yes, excitement: I'd been *right*. I ran down the driveway to the sidewalk, and then I heard the music—fast and loud with screaming guitars and steady bass, the kind of thing Angela would like. And I saw that Kendra and her mom were dancing. They reminded me of the way the Tree Frogs flailed around on stage, the unselfconsciousness that drew people to our not-very-good performances. Kendra was laughing, which I hadn't seen her do before. She and her mom were pumping their arms and legs and singing. I stood there in the glow of the streetlight with my heart pounding, watching what I realized was joy.

ACKNOWLEDGMENTS

Thank you to Christine Stroud and the team at Autumn House for improving this book and helping it to find a place in the world. I'm also grateful to Pam Houston for choosing this collection for the Autumn House Fiction Prize and for her wonderful books, which expanded my idea of what literary fiction could do. Thank you to the editors at the literary journals that originally published some of these short stories (Jonathan Bohr Heinen and Tony Varallo at *swamp pink*, Derek Askey and Andrew Snee at *The Sun*, Katie Berta and Joan Li at *The Iowa Review*, Ladette Randolph and guest editor Jamel Brinkley at *Ploughshares*). Thank you to Heidi Pitlor and Curtis Sittenfeld for including "Halloween" in *The Best American Short Stories 2020*. I have found many of my favorite short stories and writers in that anthology and look forward to it every year.

\ \ \ \ \ \ \

Thank you to the writing programs at the University of North Carolina, Arizona State University, and Florida State University and especially to my teachers Pam Durban, Melissa Pritchard, Mark Winegardner, Elizabeth Stuckey-French, and Julianna Baggott. Thank you to Loyola University Maryland for the summer grants that funded the research for this book and to my former department chair Karen Fish for encouraging me to apply for them. I am very grateful for financial support over the years from Florida State University, Arizona State University, Theresa A. Wilhoit, the Bread Loaf Writers' Conference, the Sewanee Writers' Conference, the Camargo Foundation, and Yaddo.

/ / / / / /

Thank you to my writing friends Katie Cortese and Jen Logan-Meyer who read earlier versions of these stories and helped make them much better. If you don't know their stories, please find them now. Thanks to Sophie Rosenblum for your friendship, reading suggestions, and encouragement. I'm forever grateful to those of you who met with me in Salt Lake City and Sioux Falls to talk about queer life and advocacy in your cities: in particular, Quinn Kathner, Steve Ortmeier, Tony Martinet, Mike Strayer, and Fane Harris. Thank you for your insights and for the work you do, particularly in advocating for young queer people. Thanks to Miriam DesHarnais and Lou Joseph. Thanks, too, to my father-in-law, Scott Osquist, for answering my questions about generator repair. Any errors are my own. Thank you to my talented and creative colleagues and students in the Writing Department at Loyola University Maryland.

/ / / / / /

Thank you to The Crottys (Anne, Ed, Susan, and Elizabeth) and Nesha Newton for your support of me and each other, your sense of humor, and your model of curiosity and compassion toward others. Thank you to Scott and Mary Beth Osquist for your laughter and stories, your consistent support, and your example of how to work hard while having a lot of fun. Thank you to Everett for your inquisitiveness, sense of humor, and optimism; I'm so glad you're our son. Melissa, thank you for bringing stability and adventure into my life, giving me time and space to write, providing honest feedback when I'm stuck, driving me to Chincoteague, and generally making this book (and writing life) possible.